The *NEW* Totally Awesome

MONEY BOOK

for Kids (and Their Parents)

Also by Arthur Bochner & Rose Bochner

The New Totally Awesome Business Book for Kids (and Their Parents)

By Adriane G. Berg

Moneythink

How Not to Go Broke at 102: Achieving Everlasting Wealth

Your Wealthbuilding Years

Financial Planning for Couples

Your Kids, Your Money

Gifting to People You Love

Investment Spy (CD-ROM)

Warning: Dying May Be Hazardous to Your Wealth

How to Stop Fighting About Money and Make Some

How Good Guys Grow Rich (with Milton Gralla)

Keys to Avoiding Probate and Reducing Estate Taxes

Making Up for Lost Time

The ^NEW Totally Awesome

MONEY BOOK

for Kids (and Their Parents)

Arthur Bochner & Rose Bochner

Foreword by Adriane G. Berg

Revised and Updated Third Edition

Newmarket Press

New York

This book is published in the United States of America.

ISBN: 978-1-55704-738-0

10 9 8 7 6 5 4 3 2 1

Library of Congress Cataloging-in-Publication Data

Bochner, Arthur Berg.
The totally awesome money book for kids (and their parents) /
Arthur Bochner & Rose Bochner. — 3rd ed.
p. cm.
Rev. ed. of: The totally awesome money book for kids (and their parents) /
Adriane G. Berg and Arthur Berg Bochner. 2nd ed. 2002.
Includes bibliographical references and index.
ISBN 978-1-55704-738-0 (alk. paper)

1. Finance, Personal—Juvenile literature. 2. Budgets, Personal—Juvenile
literature. I. Bochner, Rose. II. Berg, Adriane G. (Adriane Gilda), 1948-
Totally awesome money book for kids (and their parents). III. Title.
HG173.8.B65 2007
332.024—dc22
2006038930

Quantity Purchases
Companies, professional groups, clubs, and other organizations may qualify for special terms when ordering quantities of this title. For information or a catalog, write Special Sales Department, Newmarket Press, 18 East 48th Street, New York, NY 10017; call (212) 832-3575; fax (212) 832-3629;
or e-mail info@newmarketpress.com.
www.newmarketpress.com

Designed by Jaye Medalia

Manufactured in the United States of America.

This book is dedicated to

Stuart Bochner,

a k a Dad a k a Stuart Spendthrift,

and thanks for thinking up the great games.

Contents

Part 1: How to make your ideas about money grow up with you

contents

Part 2: The kids' guide: Making money with your money

contents

A word from Mom to other Moms and Dads

by Adriane G. Berg

The buck starts here.

How happy are you with the way you handle money? You'd be a major exception if you were satisfied with your money skills. In 2006 the oldest of the baby boomers turned sixty. In fact, 10,000 of us are celebrating our sixtieth birthday every day. And although we are the most educated generation in history, most of us are ill prepared to afford retirement. Too many of us are "living in our bank," having put most of our discretionary income into paying off mortgages, instead of investing.

A WORD FROM MOM

It's no secret why that has happened. We never developed a comfort zone around investing. Perhaps we rebelled against the fears of our Depression-era parents. Or perhaps we were too indulged and never expected to pay the piper. Whatever our story, it is clear that our money habits, good or bad, are the cause of our current financial situation and that those habits were derived from very early childhood experiences.

When I look at my own children, Rose (now fifteen) and Arthur (now twenty-four and the chief author of this book), and my friends' children, I see that Gen Y and X have done better. But not good enough. If you are a young parent of a young child, you still must learn about money by your wits. You certainly didn't learn much in school. This book's mission is to be sure that Web Gen members blow us out of the water when it comes to money savvy and that they, in turn, become the giving generation, because they have so much to give spiritually, financially, and intellectually.

Although this book is filled with facts to strengthen your child's money *knowledge*, I believe that the material dealing with your child's money *skills* is far more important. More important still is your child's money attitude, or money personality. In more than three decades as a money writer, journalist, and advisor, I have met numerous millionaires. I even coauthored a book with a billionaire. What made them so successful was a discipline and facility with money in all its aspects. Whether they figured their taxes, invested in real estate, ran their business, or gave to charity, it was with authority, comfort, and responsibility. They always came out ahead. You have the power to bring such ease into your child's future, whether or not you have brought it into your own.

If you work side by side with your children in reading the material in this book, you will help them achieve a level of confidence, familiarity, and perspective that is far more important than hard facts—and much harder to gain in adulthood.

And if we want our children to be confident about money handling, including investing and credit, we will have to teach them *ourselves*. Although times are changing slowly, the plain fact is that financial decision making is not taught in school, is not often taught at home, and does not come naturally. The result for most of us is lifelong anxiety and sometimes-disastrous mistakes in our money management.

Regardless of the economic times in which we live, it is always possible to earn money in America, but it's getting much harder and more complicated to invest and preserve our money. The viability of Social Security is in question, and already we must wait more years to collect the benefits we're due. Medicare is also slated to run at a deficit as Americans age. Currently, retirement is a thirty-year-long unpaid vacation. For our kids, it will be longer still. Our growing longevity is a miraculous trend, but it costs money. Like you, I want my children to have a familiarity with money that I never had growing up. When my friends and I look back on things, we agree that our ignorance about money matters was more of a handicap than was a lack of inheritance or limited earning capacity. It just takes too long to catch up when you don't begin to grasp the basics until you've already worked for several years.

In my book *Your Wealthbuilding Years*, I emphasized the

importance of early planning to those eighteen and older. But there is an even better time to start. How about fifth grade! I wish that my folks, my school, or both had paid as much attention to developing my money skills as they did to developing my social skills.

Of course, when I was a kid, Columbus was packing for his first sail. So you'd think that by now things would be different. The schools are trying, and this book's publisher hopes to share this book with many schools. There are some wonderful inroads being made in schools, but they are certainly not reaching every student. The fact is this: I had no financial education when I went to elementary school in the 1950s, Arthur had none in the 1980s, and Rose had none— and it's 2006. Rose is about to graduate from a terrific public middle school in New Jersey. She took required health education classes and even voluntary ski school, but nothing about money management was even offered.

Things are most likely the same for your children. They learn about cholesterol, free radicals, food allergies, and, of course, sex. Such information is rightly considered part of their preparation for the future. Yet not one word is spoken to prepare them to spend, save, or invest the money they will inevitably earn. There is a growing recognition of the need for attention to money matters, but only a very few children are lucky enough to receive any such basic training through their schools.

At least for now, teaching our children about money starts and stops with us. But I know how hard it is to get children, especially preteens and teens, to pay attention to our teachings.

For several years I volunteered to lecture at a children's business camp sponsored by the Foundation for Free Enterprise, part of the New Jersey State Commerce and Industry Association. It was quite an experience, preparing fifteen-year-olds to manage their money and contribute to a pension plan that would not exist for almost ten more years. They had trouble grasping the concept of retirement, were used to relying on their parents for money, and were already using credit cards! But the effort paid off. The kids loved the material and absorbed it all. But teaching one's own children is a lot different than teaching a room full of other people's kids.

In the first edition of this book, I was the coauthor with Arthur, who was then eleven years old. He does and did understand money principles very well. So does his new coauthor, Rose. Still, they are very different money people. Much of this has to do with what they absorbed indirectly from my husband and me. Every money triumph, every money fight, every money worry, and every money habit you have registers with your children, whether you realize it or not. This book has a great potential to help you reach back to your own money past and make a transformation along with your children.

But be warned: as you do so, some may criticize you for opening your children up to such "unworthy pursuits" as investing. I'll never forget when Arthur was on a television show promoting the first version of this book, and another guest (a professor, no less) argued that children would be ruined if they thought about money too early. Now that Arthur is an adult, I am proud that his security about money makes him very generous. I am happy that although he graduated with honors (and was a state finalist for the Rhodes Scholarship) and could certainly take on a high-paying job, Arthur has chosen to earn far less than he might, in order to pursue his passion by working in Washington, D.C. He shares, is not stingy, and has a healthy, optimistic attitude about the future. I see no moral downside in teaching kids about money. What Arthur knows and what I expect Rose will realize one day is that money represents the freedom to live the life you love.

Someday this book will be looked at the way we regard eighteenth-century reading primers—artifacts that taught basic knowledge at home that is today taught matter-of-factly in schools. I looked everywhere before we revised this book but still could find no book for children that taught basic economics, global investing, stock selection, credit use, and socially responsible investing at their level. Words such as *leverage, price/earnings ratio, interest,* and *creditworthy* can be understood before age thirty.

Kids easily absorb other concepts that many grown-ups still find difficult, such as mutual fund investing, dollar cost averaging, and American Depository Receipts, if those are not made into a big deal. Scientists agree that children's memory and tolerance for learning new things are much sharper than ours. Children are good at processing new ideas—better than we are. On the other hand, they have no experience of the world. They have never been fired, needed to pay for a necessity, or been faced with a week off from work without vacation pay. Most don't know what things cost. My fifteen-year-old students remind me of Dustin Hoffman's character in *Rainman,* because they can do the heaviest math but may not know the difference in cost between a house and a car.

We are going to have to be sensitive to the uneven manner in which money matters are learned. Your child will grasp some things surprisingly quickly, and you'll think you've uncovered a miniature Donald Trump. Then you'll discover that he or she thinks a mail carrier earns $1 million a year. That's why, in this book, you will find complex material that may be new to you side by side with a matching game or story.

The dual name of this book originates in the way Arthur and I first wrote it. When my publisher asked me to write a "prequel" to *Your Wealthbuilding Years*—that is, the original of this book—I took Arthur on as a sidekick. But much to my surprise, the book ended up being as much his as it was mine! We worked together on our word processor. Sometimes Arthur wrote an entire chapter and I reviewed it. Other times I engineered the ideas and then made sure he understood and could apply what I was saying. Often I showed him a real-life example of the material. For instance, in the tax chapter he learned about withholding. He understood the concept—but only when I showed him my pay stub did the horrible reality of taxation set in. As it turned out, though, there was no way I could have written the original of this book without Arthur.

And now, in the new version, I doubt that Arthur could have written this book without Rose. Nothing stays the same, and in ten years children have changed. For one thing, their Internet and computer literacy is very high. Of course, Arthur grew up with computers, but for Rose computer jargon is a first language. Because of this, children have shorter attention spans and a greater appetite for fast and visual learning. Arthur and Rose have included new material that involves the Internet, online investing, Web safety precautions, and issues of identity theft.

Still, at least some of the old techniques work. For example, very hard concepts such as the money supply, inflation, bond investing, and stock analysis are presented casually. There is no feeling that the material is too hard or just for special kids. It's no big deal. Kids should know how to read the financial section of a newspaper just as they know how to read the sports or entertainment section.

I don't expect kids to go out and buy a government bond at age twelve or start a pension plan at age fifteen, although this book teaches them how to do both. But they learn health education and sex education for their future, so why not money education, too?

We can join together to teach this without nagging and without compromising our values. Here are some things I learned that will make it easier for you to help your kids along with this book:

$ Kids have a different sense of time in relation to money. Concepts in the faraway future, such as retirement, are hard to grasp emotionally. So when explaining things such as savings, talk about immediate goals, because kids live in the present. Teenagers have a great deal to cope with right now. They are not meant to dwell on aging.

$ To kids, wealth comes from love, not from net worth. This sounds corny, but it's true. So use comfort words like **security** and **prosperity** rather than comparison words like **rich** or **poor.**

$ Some kids worry about money. Some kids worry when they learn about mortgages and collateral. They may be scared that the house they live in doesn't belong to them. Be aware that kids think deeply and that they need reassurance about money.

$ Kids like money and know more about it than you'd imagine. Kids like the feel of change in their pockets. They like to have control and pick what they want at a store. If you say no, they whine. If they are in control, they are often frugal savers. Go figure!

As a final word, I have one essential piece of advice for all parents and grandparents aspiring to making their children money mavens. When it comes to money, you are what you DO, not what you know. Your results come from the way you think, feel, and eventually act. Do take action. Open a bank account with the children, show them how you pay your bills without complaint, cherish small change and pick it up when you see it on the street, rejoice and reward them with something they really want, have them save for big items to learn patience, and never start an allowance program as a punishment or as a phony program that gives them all the money they need anyway. Be thoughtful about using the book, and they will gain an understanding far beyond knowledge, one steeped in love, joy, and mastery of money.

I have no money, I'm just a kid.

Shortsighted Sam

Arthur's introduction

I know what you're thinking: "I have no money. I'm just a kid. So why do I have to know all this money stuff?" Well, that's what I thought, too, until I found out all the benefits I could get from knowing about money. And in the years since I wrote the first version of this book with my mother, I've used my financial know-how to help me save and spend wisely.

You might think that because you don't have much money now, you don't need to know about money. But you do. You'll be handling money before you know it (if you aren't already). A person earning the minimum wage of $5.15 an hour and working a regular work week from age twenty-five to sixty-five will earn $428,480.00. That's almost half a million dollars—the minimum amount of money you and I will see in the years to come. Wow!

And the financial knowledge you can learn by reading this book can help you now just as much as in the future. If you can show your parents that you are responsible with money, they'll be more likely to trust you with it. You might get a bigger allowance or have the option to spend it on more things.

The information in this book can also help you understand what your parents are talking about when they discuss (or fight) about money. When your parents talk about money, do you sometimes not understand their discussion and feel bad about it? After reading this book, you will understand more, and you might even be allowed to take part in the conversations.

This book gives you a head start in life by making you money wise. It includes information on subjects such as borrowing, working, and even paying taxes. If you read this book, you will have a basic understanding of money. Key terms, called Moneytalk, are explained throughout the book and at the end, under "Words That Are Good to Know."

You will find out how to use a budget to help you save your money. You will learn what goals are and how to reach them. You will learn about savings and what your money can do for you.

You can also use this information to help amass a small fortune. And in other parts of the book, you will find ways to amass a large fortune through investing and lending.

Also, I think money know-how is important in helping us make a difference in the world. Chapter 13 has ideas on how you can use money responsibly to encourage a better environment and other things we care about.

My philosophy is that money is around the corner if you are looking for it. You may be able to find it more easily after you've read this book

Find the Money

Circle the words listed in the column on the left that you can find forwards and backwards, up or down. Then look for the money. Turn the page for the answer.

SCHOOLS	P	L	T	Q	M	A	S
MAGIC	R	E	H	C	A	E	T
BRIGHT	U	L	G	B	G	Z	G
	L	X	I	C	I	U	Y
TEACHER	E	P	R	L	C	U	M
RULES	S	U	B	J	E	C	T
ZEROS	A	C	Z	H	S	M	E
CHOOSE	N	P	E	R	O	H	T
	I	U	R	M	O	J	M
SUBJECT	S	L	O	O	H	C	S
TERMS	C	X	S	Z	C	O	W

A note from Rose

There is no way to avoid the issues of money when it comes to being a teenage girl. That is, I'm sure, why my brother felt he needed me to help him update this book, which he'd worked so tediously on when he was just a bit younger than I. I know that the book needs not only the cool language and styles that come with the teenage life (which Arthur hasn't experienced for years) but also the presence of a female voice.

There is so much to learn about money and investing that I could not possibly have survived this far without the knowledge I now have. Without the help from my brother, my mother, and this book, my wallet and bank account could not satisfy my need for clothes, music, hair products, and the ever-inflating price of movie tickets (and I wouldn't have been able to save so much for college). I'm constantly reminded about saving my money, investing my money, and (my personal favorite) spending my money. There is a lot to remember about all of these things, and you will find information about them all in this book.

Answer:
It's a Dollar Sign = $

```
        T   M
R E H C A E T
  U   G   G
  L   I   I
  E   R   C
S U B J E C T
    Z   S   E
    E   O   R
    R   O   M
S L O O H C S
    S   C
```

PART 1

How to make your ideas about money grow up with you

You already know a lot more about money than you think or than some grown-ups realize. Most of you buy a school lunch and know the price. Some of you already have a job, get an allowance, and even make investments.

Maybe you've gotten a gift from your grandparents and wanted to spend it on a toy or game, but your folks had you put it away for savings instead. Maybe your folks, like many other parents, bought a piggy bank when you were still a baby and, over time, taught you about keeping change. All the popular TV and cartoon characters have money-related toys to sell, such as the "character banks" made by Sesame Street, Disney, and Mattel.

Not only do you know something about saving and spending, but if you are like most other kids, you are an aware consumer, too. On the back of your cereal box there may be a coupon to get money back. Your town may have a law that requires a deposit on soda cans and bottles and gives a refund when they are returned. Maybe you already look for sales or buy toys at garage sales or on the Internet.

Your parents may talk about money in the home—to you or to each other. There may be discussions and even fights

$3.00 Rebate!

Get three (3) $1.00 checks back by mail when you send in this offer form along with 6 proofs-of-purchase from any 3 different cereal products. Mail this form to: Cereal Company, 123 Wheat Street, Barley, IA 67890

NAME _____

ADDRESS _____

CITY_____ STATE _____ ZIP _____

Void where prohibited by law. Offer expires 12/25/2007

about money taking place around you. If you or an older brother or sister is near college age, the cost of school is surely a topic of conversation.

As you grow up, money will take on a bigger role in your life. Someday you will be the mom or dad who supports the family, makes the money decisions, and keeps everyone in the family fed, clothed, and housed.

It's important for the ideas you have about money to grow up as you do. One childish thing that stops many grown-ups from feeling comfortable with money is the idea that to be good with money you must be good with math. Money has nothing to do with math, whether you like math or not. Many grown-ups shy away from money management because they don't think they are good at math. Their money habits didn't mature with them.

While it's important to know how to add and subtract, you can get the idea of how money works in your life without being a math genius. To give you a better head start than most grown-ups have, part 1 gives you a grasp of where your money comes from now and later, shows you the importance of setting goals, and even begins you on a budget and savings plan.

And you can learn and do all this even if you're not handling any money now. Did your mom or dad ever buy you clothes that were a little too big so you could wear them for a long time while you grew? Well, this book is like that. Some of the ideas are a little too big for some of you to use right now, but you will grow into them and then have the tools you need when the time comes to make bigger money decisions. In that way, your ideas about money will grow along with you.

CHAPTER 1

$

Money:

Where does it come from, anyway?

When you find a penny on the street or you watch your mom pay for something at the store, do you ever wonder where the money comes from? Why are these coins and paper the things we use to trade for the stuff we want? How do we get money and keep it? How come some people have more money than others have?

economists at work

The mint

Believe it or not, each country, including the United States, makes its own money. The factory where our money is manufactured is called the *mint*. It's located in Washington, D.C., and you and your family can take a free tour if you ever visit the capital. You can also learn all kinds of neat facts about our money by visiting the U.S. Mint's kid-friendly Web site: www.usmint.gov/kids.

If you do, you'll see how coins are cast and paper money is printed. You will also see how old bills are destroyed. There are heavy security checks to make sure no one takes any of the newly minted money or the old money slated for destruction.

Counting all the money in the United States

Our own government, mostly through an agency called the *Fed* (short for *Federal Reserve Board*), makes the decision about how much money to manufacture. The people who work for the Fed, such as the board's chairman, regularly take a count of all the money in circulation. They check out how much is in bank accounts and other places where people like your parents keep their money. They check out how banks are lending money and whether it's easy or hard to get money.

keeping

making

getting

money juggler

They add up all the money out there and call the total *M-1*. If M-1 is low, they can actually print more money or do other things to encourage banks to lend money and you to borrow.

If there is too much money out there, sometimes prices go up. Maybe you know the word *inflation*. It means things are getting too expensive because there is a lot of money around and people will pay high prices. When there is inflation, the Fed can make the money supply tighter to counteract it.

In our country, we each control the money in coins and paper that comes our way. The more of it we keep, the wealthier we are. The less we have, the less wealthy. So far, we are the wealthiest country in the whole world. But remember that wealth comes from three things: getting money in the first place, keeping the money in the second place, and then making the money grow.

As you get older, you get better at doing all three, like a skilled juggler. Kids often think that the hardest part is getting the money in the first place. Arthur can't remember getting any money until he was nine. And then he got it only because he collected his father's change.

Since he started working, he really learned a lot about where money comes from and how to keep it and make it grow. Here are all the ways we can think of how people, even kids, can get money. Can you think of any more?

§ **Earn it with a job** such as delivering groceries or newspapers.

§ **Earn it in a business** such as a lemonade stand.

§ **Trade for it** with something you have, like a baseball card.

§ **Find it** in the street.

§ **Win it** in a game.

§ **Get a gift.**

§ **Get a scholarship** or an award for doing something well.

§ **Get a refund** or a rebate for bringing something back to a store like soda bottles or cans.

§ **Sell old collectibles** on eBay.

§ **Sell old books** on eBay or Amazon.com.

CHAPTER 1
$

• • • • • • • • • • • • • • •

The M-1 Poem

There was an old Fed
With money to spread
Who made an old banker a loan.
Along came a man
With a big moving van
And was able to buy an old home.
He needed some paint
So his wife wouldn't faint,
So he hired a boy with a brush.
When I pay you today,
put the money away.
You'll increase the M-1 in a rush.

• • • • • • • • • • • • • • •

If you keep any of this money that comes your way in a bank, it's counted as part of the nation's money supply. So your bank account, your parents' bank account, and your teacher's bank account are all part of M-1—awesome!

Actually, all our money is connected. If there is lots of it, people spend. If they spend, businesses do well. If businesses do well, more people have jobs. They then have more money to spend. In Moneytalk, this is called a *recovery* or an *economic expansion*.

It goes the other way, too. With less money around, there is less spending, less business, and fewer jobs. This is called a *recession*. Our mom has lived through eight recessions since 1954, which shows that the economy changes all the time. It goes in cycles, and we must realize that times change for good and bad and that we should be prepared for both.

The circulation of money

Money has two sides, just like a coin. Think of money as heads and tails. Heads you earn; tails you spend. But the weird part about it is that every time you spend, another person earns what you spent.

When you buy a juice box for a dollar, you pay the storekeeper for it. You spent, and he earned. Then, when the storekeeper wants to buy something for himself, he will spend your dollar. The person he buys from will earn it. This shows us how money stays in circulation all the time.

The Heads-and-Tails Money Game

Play this simple game and you will see for yourself:

Give each player five pennies. Make one team Heads and the other team Tails. Flip a quarter. If it lands on heads, the Heads team gets a penny from the Tails team. If it lands on tails, the Tails team gets a penny from the Heads team. Keep track of how many times you can play before one team earns all the coins.

The tossing of the coin can result in one team winning with as few as 5 tosses. More likely, it will take as many as 25 or even 50 tosses before one team wins. It can go on forever, with an infinite number of tosses. A game with a lot of tosses is like a healthy national economy. Things stay moving. The same currency (money) is spent and respent by all the people.

Money keeps moving in a healthy economy. When people get afraid to spend because they are afraid they won't earn, the system breaks down and the economy doesn't grow or even shrinks. (Another way to think about a recession, which we defined earlier, is as a long period of economic shrinkage.)

The grand total of all the money spent in a nation on goods and services is called the *gross domestic product (GDP)*. This number is a good measure of the wealth of a country. (The GDP of the United States in 2005 was roughly $12 trillion, making our nation the world's wealthiest.) Now, if people stop spending, other people stop making things to buy. The GDP gets smaller, and the country gets poorer. It's like a quick game in which one side gets all the pennies fast and the game stops—no fun.

But even in a slow economy, some people have enough money. That's because they know how to do some extra things to help money come their way.

Things you can do to help money come your way

Money won't come to you in all the ways we've mentioned all the time, but we found that it helps to be on the lookout. We all have friends who are very different when it comes to money. Some think about it, and some don't. Some try to learn about money, and some find it boring. It doesn't matter; they're all great kids. But one thing is certain: the kids who pay attention to money seem to have more of it.

Eventually, we will all work, and money will come our

The Money I Have Now

(also called your *gross assets*—how's that for Moneytalk?):

$ _____ Amount

I got it from:

_____ Gift   _____ Won it

_____ Allowance   _____ Refund

_____ Found it   _____ Rebate

_____ Earned it   _____ Return
on an investment

way. The trouble is that money comes, but it also goes. Sometimes money gets spent so fast that grown-ups have to start all over every week from scratch. If that happens, they never get any wealth, no matter how much money comes their way.

But the good thing about money is that even when it goes, it can come back and stay awhile. Two stories about famous Americans can teach us how important it is to save.

The first story is about a boy named Abe. His parents had very little money come their way. So Abe decided to work hard and put himself through school. He became a lawyer. He learned how to make his money grow. Eventually, he got an important job and stayed wealthy. That boy was Abraham Lincoln. Saving really can make a difference in your life.

The second story teaches the same lesson. A boy named George was also poor. His parents put him in an orphanage. He became an athlete and made even more money than the president of the United States. But he didn't know how to

Here are some of the things our friends do to have money come their way:

$ **Take soda cans back** to the store to get a 5-cent refund.

$ **Work.** (A girl Arthur knows is an actress, and a boy Rose knows gives tennis lessons to younger kids. Others have paper routes and mow lawns.)

$ **Start a business.**

$ **Pick up a penny.** (There was once a **Candid Camera** show where no one even bothered to pick up a dime they saw on the street. It must not have meant much to the grown-ups. Our friends would probably pick it up. Would you?)

$ **The more grateful you are,** the more money will come to you. When you do pick up money or are given it as a gift, say, "Hooray, I am lucky" and feel grateful. Gratitude is to money what water is to a flower—something that makes it grow and grow.

keep that money. Pretty soon, there wasn't much left. George's middle name was Herman, but everyone called him Babe—Babe Ruth.

The point is that people aren't just rich or poor. Money doesn't stay away or stay put. You control what happens to the money that comes your way. You can start right now by paying attention to how much money you have and figuring out where it comes from. Add up how much you have today. Is it 25 cents, 25 dollars, or even more? However much it is, the money is yours. It does what you want it to do. That's why goals are so important, even to us kids. Let's look at goals in the next chapter.

Goals:

What do you want from the money in your life?

If you know exactly what you want, you're halfway to getting it.

Gail Goalsetter

A *goal* is something you want for yourself or someone you love. It's a target, a thing you want to achieve. Anything from the toys you would like to own to the college you would like to attend can be a goal. Money is useful to meet your goals. Sometimes, all you need is the money, like when your goal is to go to a movie. Other times, money is only part of a goal, like when you want to start a business.

So to get what you really want from the money in your life, it's important to set goals and know how much they cost. When you do this, here are some of the good things that happen:

$ **You don't waste money** on things you don't want.

$ **You can give up the things** that are less important to get the things that are more important.

$ **You can go on to the next goal** when you reach your first goal.

$ **You are happy** even if you are working hard, because you anticipate the reward you will get.

Cheap and expensive goals

There are two types of goals: things that you want right away and things that are for the future. In Moneytalk, the ones you want now are called *short-term goals*. The future ones are called *long-term goals*.

Some long-term goals are attending college, retiring, buying a house, and opening a business. Some short-term goals are going to the movies, buying a bike, buying Christmas gifts for the family, or having money for a school trip. Most long-term goals, such as attending college, cost a lot of money. But so do some short-term goals. Many teenagers want a car as soon as they learn to drive. It's a short-term goal, but it's expensive. Still, short-term goals are usually cheaper and faster to save for than long-term goals are. Sometimes you must give up short-term goals to reach your long-term goals. No one we know gets all the short- and long-term goals they want, but there is a way to get many of them. The way is by making a *plan*.

Turning a wish into a goal by making a plan

When you first think about long-term and short-term goals, they are just a bunch of wishes. But if you make a plan to reach them, you can turn a wish into a goal that you can achieve.

Here are some short-term goals:

$ Buying a necklace

$ Buying an Xbox

$ Buying a DVD

$ Buying a watch

$ Buying an iPod

Here are some long-term goals:

$ Attending college

$ Being a lawyer

$ Going to vet school

$ Buying a house

$ Buying a car

$ Getting married

$ Buying an apartment

$ Retiring at sixty

So, the first money basic is this: *List your wishes; then make a plan. A plan turns a wish into a goal that you are able to achieve.* Some people at Harvard University did a study in which they visited graduates years after they'd left the university. Along with their great education, all had good jobs or businesses, but the ones with a written plan did many times better in having money and wealth than those with no written plan. So, once you pick a goal, write it down and make a plan!

Remember the difference between goals, plans, and

wishes. A goal is your target, the thing you want. A plan is the way you intend to reach your goal and get what you want. A wish is something you want but have no plan to get. Without a plan, wishes often don't come true. With a plan, a wish becomes a goal in your control.

List some of your wishes now. After reading about budgets in chapter 3, you'll see how you can reach them by setting goals and making a plan.

My wishes are: _____

My goals are: _____

My plans are: _____

Here's a quiz to see if you know the difference between a wish, a goal, and a plan. Put **G** for goal, **W** for wish, and **P** for plan:

_____ 1. Owning all the video games in the store

_____ 2. Saving to buy an iPod

_____ 3. Owning a video game, like Halo 2

_____ 4. Going to college

_____ 5. Working to pay for college

_____ 6. Getting all As at college

_____ 7. Buying a tie for Dad

_____ 8. Buying Dad a present

_____ 9. Finding a clothing sale

Be careful what you wish for, you might get it! Don't save for a puppy if you really won't care for it.

Pablo Payment

When what you want is almost impossible or very unnecessary, it's probably just a wish (owning all the video games in the store). When you know exactly what you want, you have a goal (owning Halo 2). When you know what you must do to get it, you have a plan (saving).

Some things are wishes that can become goals. Getting all As in college is a wish. But once you get to college, you can make it a goal by having a study program.

Some things are just wishes because they are not clear enough in your mind (buying Dad a present). If they get clear, they are goals (buying a tie for Dad).

As you keep reading this book, come back to this chapter and add wishes, plans, and goals. Maybe you have already reached some of your goals. Make a list of them right now.

Goals I've already made:_____

No matter how old you are now, you will always have new goals all your life. And you will always have to make new plans. So the sooner you get used to those facts, the better.

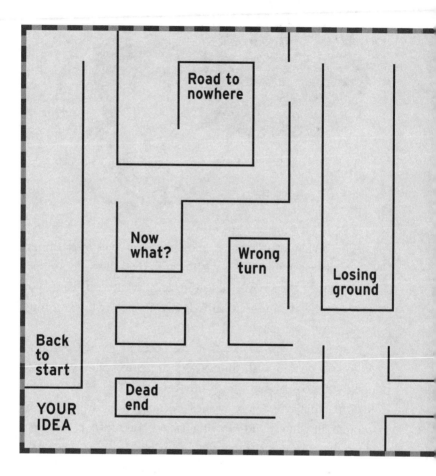

The Maze of Success

From now on, instead of thinking you can have everything or can't have anything, make plans for the things that are really important and stick with them. One type of plan that involves money is a savings plan. We'll talk about this in the next chapter.

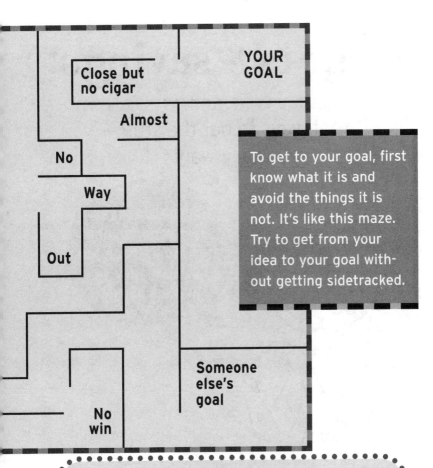

Close but no cigar

YOUR GOAL

Almost

No

Way

Out

To get to your goal, first know what it is and avoid the things it is not. It's like this maze. Try to get from your idea to your goal without getting sidetracked.

Someone else's goal

No win

Things to Do

Here are some questions to ask your parents:

- $ What are their goals?
- $ What achievements are they most proud of?
- $ Which are the hardest goals to reach?
- $ What were their goals when they were your age?

Budgets & savings:

Great ways to get the stuff you really want

Budgets are for everyone. No one has too little or too much money to make a budget.

What is a budget?

A budget is a way of keeping track of the money you get and the money you spend. When you know how much things cost and how you are spending your money, lots of good things happen.

For example, if you know that candy costs 50 cents at the drugstore, you won't pay 75 cents to a candy machine. Also, by having an idea of how much you have to spend, you won't fall into the trap of overspending. With a budget, you won't use up your allowance by the middle of the week and have to ask for more money or go without the stuff you want.

And the super thing about a budget is that it helps you get all the things you really want. It shows you how much of your money is spent on junk you don't need or want. Finally, a budget helps you save for the expensive things that you can't afford to buy right away.

How come some people don't use budgets?

Some people give budgets a bad rap because they think that budgeting makes you give up the things that make you happy. They think a budget is like a diet, where you have to stop yourself from having fun. Just the opposite is true. Let's look at what happened when a boy named Thomas made a budget and how he got everything he wanted.

Thomas's totally awesome budget

Fourteen-year-old Thomas was always running out of money. There was a long list of stuff he wanted and couldn't have. He often got into trouble because of this. For example, one day he spent the class-trip money his father gave him on extra candy. Then he sold his favorite baseball card in order to make the trip money back. Thomas didn't enjoy the candy,

America's Annual Budget

$ Housing = $13,918

$ Food and drink = $5,781

$ Clothing and services = $1,816

$ Transportation=$7,801

$ Healthcare = $2,574

This is the budget for a family that earns $54,453 before taxes. Add up the expenses and then deduct those from the income. After this family pays taxes, what's left over is what the family can save. (These numbers come from a 2004 study by the Bureau of Labor Statistics, a federal agency.)

missed his baseball card, and was miserable during the class trip. Can this boy be saved? *Yes. With a budget!*

To make a budget, the first thing you should do is write down all the money that you get from anyone, in any form. All gifts, allowance, and payments for work are included. Don't bother with money you find only once in a while. You can't count on that every week. All this money you get is called *income,* in Moneytalk.

Here is Thomas's income:

$ **$5.00 a day,** school lunch money.................$25.00
(5 days x $5.00)

$ **$10.00 a week,** allowance every Saturday........$10.00

$ **$5.00 a week,** lawn-mowing income................$5.00

If we add this all up, we find that Thomas's income each week is $40.00. When Thomas did the math, he was shocked at how much income he had. It was even more puzzling that he never had enough money. This was because Thomas didn't keep track of his spending.

Next, you should write down all the things you spend on. This total is what living costs you. It's called the *cost of living* or your *expenses*. When Thomas did the second part of the budget, the mystery was solved.

Here are Thomas's expenses:

$ **$5.50 a day for school lunch** (The price of the school lunch went up by 50 cents; but Thomas never paid any attention, so he never told his parents that the price had increased.)

$ **$2.50 a day for after-school snack** (Because his friend Jim ordered the special every day, Thomas also bought the special at the pizzeria. It was two slices and a soda for $2.50. Thomas ate only one slice and threw the other one away. That means Thomas spent all of his after-school snack and mowing money on something he threw away each day.)

And now it's time to take a third step, the list that most people who make budgets forget to do. Thomas was ready to make a list of the things he really wanted.

Thomas wanted:

$ an MP3 player $ another Xbox game
$ a new pair of Vans shoes

How Do You Feel?

How do you feel when other kids have more money to spend than you do? Does it make a difference if they are your close friends? If so, why? And how do you feel when other kids have less money to spend than you do? Does it make a difference if they are your close friends? If so, why?

"Wow," thought Thomas, "I'll never get that awesome stuff." He realized that he spent his extra money on gum, baseball cards, and other cheap stuff because what he really wanted was so expensive he never believed he could get it. Without a budget, he would have just spent his money on quick substitutes for his real dreams. Look what Thomas did with his budget. First, he told his parents that the price of a school lunch had increased. They gave him the extra 50 cents each day. Next, he stopped buying the pizza special. Instead, he bought one slice for $1.50 and took an extra juice from home. Making those changes saved Thomas $7.50 a week, and he and Jim are still pals.

Thomas started to concentrate on the things he really wanted. After getting permission from his parents, he found a used MP3 player on eBay for a very low price. Also, Thomas told everyone he knew about the Xbox game he wanted and asked if they knew where to buy one cheaply. Within a week, a girl named Judy offered to trade her game in return for a few CDs plus $14.00 in cash.

It was a fair deal for both of them. Instead of spending

$50.00 on a new game, Thomas spent $14.00 and traded some of his duplicate cards. Judy got rid of a game she was tired of and got some money and cards she really wanted.

Finally, the Vans were the only thing left on Thomas's most-wanted list. Thomas's income was $42.50 a week. But his expenses were much less. Lunch and snacks cost him $35.00 a week. With the extra money, Thomas decided to save $7.50 a week for the sneakers. It took him ten weeks to buy the sneakers, but he enjoyed wearing them very much.

Balancing a budget

Budgeting is like playing on a teeter-totter. It should balance on both sides. Cutting down on expenses can be just as helpful as adding money.

The Teeter-Totter Riddle
Try this balancing feat:

Four friends are playing on the teeter-totter. John weighs 90 pounds and Mary weighs 60 pounds, for a total of 150 pounds on the right side. Leroy weighs 80 pounds and David, 70; they balance the left side at 150 pounds.

Now rearrange the friends when Jesus, who weighs 40 pounds, wants to play. Can you do it?

Just put Leroy and John together and David, Mary, and Jesus on the other side for balance. Each side is now 170 pounds, and they balance.

Now Balance Your Own Budget

Here are some things you should include in your budget.

List your income:

- $ Weekly allowance
- $ Lunch money
- $ Job 1
- $ Job 2
- $ Other
- $ Once in a while
- $ Gifts
- $ Bonus
- $ Other

List your expenses:

- $ Food
- $ Transportation
- $ School trips
- $ Snacks
- $ Toys
- $ Clothes
- $ Gifts for others
- $ Other

Take your income and subtract your expenses. Are you over or under your budget? Or are you even?

If you are under budget, save that extra money. If you spend more than you take in, start a plan to spend less and add savings to your weekly income.

CHAPTER 4

$

Budgets:

How to get more of those great savings

The best way to get more money to spend on the things you want is to make a budget for the money you have.

Responsible Rhoda

If you think about Thomas's story, you'll see how many things he learned from budgeting. Here are a few things you can learn about your own money with a budget:

$ **How much income are you getting?** Where does it come from? How can you increase it?

$ **Where is your money going?** Can you get the same things cheaper? Are the things worth the money? Are you getting what you really want?

$ **What do you really want?** Can you get it for free? Can you borrow it? Can you trade for it?

$ **How long will it take** to save for it?

Above all, Thomas learned that budgets are a personal thing. What stuff you want is up to you and your parents. He didn't have to eat what Jim ate, and he didn't have to want what Judy wanted. And if you want to be like everyone else, that's okay, too. When you save with a budget, you are not stopping yourself from getting what you want. Just the opposite. You are *taking control* of your money so you can *get what you want.*

Two types of budgets–
for kids who are spenders and
kids who are savers

Penelope and Sammy go to the toy store

Penelope Pennypincher and Sammy Spender go to the toy store. Each has $20.00 to spend. They look around. Penelope says, "I like this game, but it costs $10.95. That's too expensive. I've seen it for $9.00 in another store. I won't spend this much." Sammy says, "You're silly. Why wait? Is it worth saving $1.95 to miss out on playing the game this afternoon? Anyway, I like this game that costs $19.99. Since I have $20.00, I'm going to buy it.

"Now hurry up and pick something," says Sammy. But Penelope leaves the store without buying anything. Penelope has the whole $20.00 left and no game. Sammy has a game and no money left over (he even had to ask his parents for some extra money to pay the sales tax on the game).

Which of these kids is more like you? Was there a right or wrong attitude? Which of them would you rather know and feel comfortable with?

I say, "A penny saved is a penny earned." Sammy Spender says, "Live for today—tomorrow will take care of itself."

What do you say?

Penelope Pennypincher

Some kids like to keep records and put down everything they get and spend. Others don't like to. They forget or get bored. Still, everyone needs to have a budget. If you are the kind of kid who likes to keep track of money, use the form at the end of chapter 3 every month. Each day, keep a record of income and expenses to enter on your budget form.

A budget for kids who like to spend money but hate to keep track

If you don't like all that pencil-and-paper action, there is a special trick. And even if you are a kid who likes to keep track, you could try this once because it gives you a different kind of look at how you spend your money.

Just once, do the following things:

$ Make a list of what you spend your money on.

$ Write down the amount you spend, as best as you can, on each item.

$ List which are costs you can't change, like school lunch.

$ List those costs you can change, like a snack.

$ Take those that you can control and list them in order of the ones you like most.

Here's Rose's list:

$ crossword magazine $ gum $ soda

By doing this, you know what you are spending and what you can eliminate because it is not important to you. Stop spending on the last thing or two on the list. Just cut them out altogether. You'll never miss them.

If you still don't have the money for the things you really want, go up the list and stop spending on all the things that are not important. If it's still not enough, shop around to get things cheaper.

And finally, if you still can't get all the stuff you want, you'll have to wait and save up for it. When you put away the money you spend on the stuff you don't need or like so you can get something better, this is called *savings*, in Moneytalk.

Most kids save for things they can see, such as toys. Most grown-ups save for things they can't see, like "a rainy day" when they'll need the money for an emergency. But either way, the money is still yours, so you can get what you want later.

Things I spend money on that I control:

1. _____
2. _____
3. _____
4. _____
5. _____
6. _____

**Things from the previous list that
I can't live without:**

1. _____
2. _____
3. _____

**Things that are great but I could
do without:**

1. _____
2. _____
3. _____

Things I spend on that I can cut out:

1. _____
2. _____
3. _____

Making the most of your savings

By now, you know that a budget helps you save money so you can get what you really want in the future. It makes you richer and doesn't deprive you of anything. Since saving is so good, why do most people find it so hard to do?

Most people find it hard to save because they want everything right away. You can get just about all you want, but not immediately. Have you ever noticed how babies cry when they don't get a bottle as soon as they want one? Even big kids and grown-ups feel that way about getting things *now!* If you can feel better about waiting for what you want, you will save more and get better things later.

Penelope Pennypincher and Sammy Spender can work together to save money.

How to make saving money easier

Every time you get money, put some away immediately. Just put it in a drawer or piggy bank. Another great way to save and set aside your money for specific purposes is to separate it into envelopes, files, or jars marked with labels, such as Long Term, Short Term, Gifts, Savings, Charity, or anything else that might mean something to you.

Shopping for interest rates

The younger you are when you start to save, the more your money grows by the time you are twenty-one, for instance. Banks will actually pay you to save your money with them. They give you a percentage of the money you keep at their bank every year. This percentage is called *interest*. Remember, when you visit a bank, you are their customer. You shouldn't be afraid to ask questions—the people at the bank want your business. They believe that if you start banking with them while you're young, you'll stay with them as you get older and need more financial services. This makes you very powerful at a young age!

Take a look at how money grows if you start as a kid. Here's how putting $1,000 in a bank will grow at given interest rates (that added money given to you by the bank) until you are twenty-one.

Your starting age now, with $1,000 annual deposit:

% Interest Rate	A New Baby	7	11	16	20
		TOTAL EARNED BY AGE 21:			
5%	$34,719	$22,657	$13,207	$5,802	$1,050
8%	$49,423	$29,324	$15,645	$6,336	$1,080
11%	$71,265	$38,190	$18,561	$6,913	$1,110
14%	$103,769	$49,980	$22,045	$7,536	$1,140
17%	$152,139	$65,649	$26,200	$8,207	$1,170
20%	$224,026	$86,442	$31,150	$8,930	$1,200

As you see, interest is always a percentage, so a 5 percent interest rate means that you will get five extra pennies for every dollar you've lent to the bank (that is, put on deposit there). Interest is credited—added to your account—every month, half-year, or year, depending on the bank or other borrower.

The best deal for you is having interest credited every month. Why? Because if your interest also is earning interest (which is called *compounding*), the interest is added on faster. That means the money you've earned is earning money itself!

So start saving early. Also, you can see that the higher the interest rate, the better you will do. So you should shop around for a good rate. Here's how:

$ **Ask the bank** how often it credits your interest.

$ **Get a chart** of the rates they offer.

$ **Find out if they pay less** on small accounts.

$ **Find out if they skip holidays** in giving interest.

$ **Find out whether, if you take out money** before the end of the year, you still get interest up to the day you took it out. This is called **day-of-deposit to day-of-withdrawal crediting.**

$ **Find out whether the bank charges** you any money if you don't keep putting money in regularly.

$ **Find out if you can view** your account online through the bank's Web site for free or if that access costs money.

$ **Find out if there are any other fees** tied to the account.

PART 2

The kids' guide: Making money with your money

Remember our juggler in chapter 1? One of the balls he tried to keep up in the air was called "making," for "making money grow."

You can get money through gifts, earnings, and other ways. You have just read about keeping your money by using goals, budgets, and savings. But a very hard job that you will eventually have is using your saved money to make even more money. Why do we need to do this?

There are two reasons it's important that you use your saved money to earn more money. The first is that one day you will stop working. This is called *retirement*. It's pretty hard to imagine retiring even before you have had your first job. But retirement is a time when you have enough money that's making more money for you so that you don't have to work. You might work anyway, but you don't have to.

The second reason that money must make money is inflation. Remember, that's when things cost more to buy. Some-

times prices go up more than your earnings from a job. Your money needs to earn money so you can keep up with the cost of living.

A lot of grown-ups think that making money grow is even harder than earning it in the first place or keeping it in the second place. There is a good explanation for this. Every time you try to have your money make money for you, you must take a risk. The risk is that you will lose it. However, if you refuse to take any risk, your money will never grow.

To make money, you must take a little risk; to make more, a bigger risk. But it is pretty hard to judge whether the risk is right and worthwhile. Some people are more comfortable with risk than others. You have to decide for yourself by trying different things out. It's good to get used to the idea now, before you have to put a lot of real money on the line.

CHAPTER 6
$
The risks & rewards of moneymaking

If you got money and budgeted to save it, you would then like to see it grow. Even without earning, finding, winning, borrowing, or getting money as a gift, you can end up with more.

You already understand that interest is added to your savings if you put them in a real bank instead of a piggy bank. When you use your money to make more money, it's called *investing*. The original amount you saved is called *capital*.

The amount added to it by investing is called *growth*.

With the help of your parents, you can make money with your money. You don't need a lot to start with. Many investments can be made with just $25. If you make the right choice, you'll end up with much more. But it's important to know that sometimes when you invest capital, you can lose your money! So let's see how investments work.

There are only two kinds of investing. Both are ways that your money can make money, but they are very different.

One way that your money makes money is *lending it to others in return for interest* (extra money they pay you for the right to borrow your money). This is usually very safe and sure. You get a stated amount of money back on a specific date. For example, if you lend your brother $10.00, and he promises to give you back $11.00, you have just made a deal to be paid an extra dollar. That is what it cost him to borrow your money. Stated in a percentage, that's a 10 percent interest rate.

Another way you can use your money to make more money is by *buying something today that may be worth more tomorrow and then selling it*. For example, if you buy a baseball card for $1.00 and resell it later for $1.50, that's called a *profit*. When you buy stocks (shares of ownership in a company), you also hope that you will sell those later at a profit. By waiting until the value goes up, your money can make a lot more money this way than by lending. But you can also lose money or make less. It's a risk. You'll learn a lot more about stocks in a later chapter.

Our mom says that the hardest thing for grown-ups to understand is that money is always risked, at least a little,

when you use it to make more money. Some grown-ups take too much risk and some too little. But either way, it makes most of them uncomfortable. Adults take risks anyway, because the most money can be made from the riskiest investments. If they have extra money they can afford to lose, they may even take big chances, called *speculation*.

Some investments are absolutely safe, like lending your money to the U.S. government when you buy a savings bond. Others involve risks, like buying stocks. We will read about both. Different types of risk-and-reward combinations are right for different people and even for the same person at different times in his or her life.

The Totally Awesome Risk/Reward Game for Kids

(and their parents)

Here's a fun way to see how different risks bring different rewards. You can play this game a hundred times and never come out with exactly the same result. All you need is a single die.

Each player can begin on any Start space. When it is your turn, roll the die and move the number of spaces it says. Follow the instructions on the space on which you landed. The first player to finish wins.

start 1	back to start		lose turn				go to end		back to start	
start 2	lose turn		lose turn		back to start		go to end		lose turn	
start 3		lose turn	move ahead 2 spaces	lose turn		go back 1 space		move ahead 2 spaces	lose turn	
start 4			go back 1 space		lose turn		go back 1 space			lose turn
start 5										

Who won when you played? Was it the player who started on Path 1, the most risky? He or she could be sent back to Start. Or was the winner the one who took Path 5, the longest path but the one with no risk? Or did the player who started on Path 2, 3, or 4, with a different mix of length and risk, win?

The more times you play, the more you will get different results. That's just like money. There are many roads to success and many combinations of risk (lose a turn) and reward (go to end). Which player would you like to be? The winner who takes the most risk? The winner who takes longer and has no risk? Or the one who takes a combination of risk and reward?

back to start	lose turn			go to end		back to start			end 1
lose turn	lose turn		back to start	go to end		lose turn			end 2
lose turn	move ahead 2 spaces	lose turn		go back 1 space		move ahead 2 spaces	lose turn		end 3
	go back 1 space		lose turn		go back 1 space			lose turn	end 4
									end 5

Making money by lending your money to others

O ne way to invest is to lend your money to others. They use your money for something they want, and then they give you back more money than you gave them. They are paying you for the chance to use your money for a while.

This is exactly what happens when you put money in a bank. When you open an account with $10 of your money, it will grow without you doing anything more. This happens because the bank pays you interest. Why does a bank pay you for leaving money with it?

Here's the secret: Your ten dollars isn't really sitting in the account. The bank is using your money by investing it and making money for itself. This means the bank wants to use your money for as long as you let it. To get the use of your

money, it will pay you. Lots of kids feel afraid or intimidated in a bank. It was built for grown-ups, and sometimes the building looks very big. But when you walk into a bank to put money in an account, even if it is one penny, you are the boss. You are lending your money to the bank, and the bank wants something you have. There are lots of banks, but there is only one you. And remember that any bank wants you as a lifelong client!

It's much easier to win at moneymaking when your eyes are wide open.

The Bull's-Eye Game

Try this Bull's-Eye game. Take a coin. Close your eyes. Try to flip the coin into one of the circles with your eyes closed. Almost impossible! Now flip it with your eyes open. I bet you did better. Finally, keep your eyes open and place the coin in the center. You can't miss!

It's the same with investment decisions: keeping your eyes open is like having knowledge. Placing instead of flipping is like taking it easy, taking your time, and not getting pushed into a decision too fast.

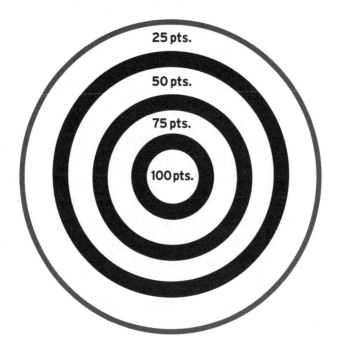

CDs

CD is Moneytalk for **certificate of deposit.** It's a way of lending money to a bank for a period of time, from a month to five years, in return for interest. The downside is you can't get your money back until the end of the CD's term. On the upside, however, you can get a better interest rate than you would in a regular savings or checking account.

Things to know before you lend your money

Before you lend your money to a bank or to anyone else, there are some things you should find out:

How safe is your money? When you lend your capital (money), you want it back someday. Money in banks is very safe because even if the bank goes out of business, the federal government will make sure you get your money back. This is called *FDIC insurance. FDIC* stands for *Federal Deposit Insurance Corporation,* which is an agency of the U.S. government set up in 1933 to pay you back your money if the bank can't.

How safe is the interest you are getting? After all, you are lending your money to the bank for a reason. The reason is to get interest added to your dollars. To be sure that you will really get what you expect, you want a promise that the interest will be paid. This promise is called a *guarantee.* The federal government also guarantees your interest with FDIC insurance. Everyone is insured up to $100,000, so I don't think

Money Riddles

Q. Why is Washington, D.C., like the money you put in the bank?

A. Because they are both called the capital.

Q. Why do you never get bored when you put your money in a bank?

A. Because it keeps giving you interest.

Q. Why does your bond get serious when you cash it in?

A. Because it reached its maturity date.

we kids have to worry.

When will you get your money back? When you lend money, you can make different arrangements about when you get it back. In most cases, you can take your money back whenever you want it. Doing this is called making a *withdrawal.* The bank can't stop you. You get back all your capital plus any interest you've earned on your money. But you can also arrange to let the bank keep your money until a certain date. You can't ask for it back before then, even if you need it. The date when you can get back the money is called the *maturity date,* in Moneytalk. Usually you will get a higher percentage of interest if you promise not to take back the money before a certain date.

How much money will your money make? What you are really asking, in Moneytalk, is, "How much interest will my capital earn?" That depends. Anyone who wants to borrow your money wants to pay you as little as possible. Don't get mad, since that's just good business. The amount they pay in interest depends on some complicated economic things, such as how much they can make by using your money and how much other banks are willing to pay.

CHAPTER 8

$

Who wants to borrow a kid's money?

You'd be surprised!

Banks are not the only businesses that want to borrow your money. You'll be surprised to find out how many ways there are to lend your money in return for interest. Sometimes it's hard to decide which one you want to do business with. In this chapter we tell you about some other ways to make money by lending your money.

Things to Do

To get more information about U.S. government bonds, visit **www.savingsbonds.gov**. You can learn more about bonds, and even buy some online.

The U.S. Government

The U.S. (or federal) government wants to borrow your money in return for giving you interest. If you lend it your money, you get proof of the loan by getting a Series EE bond, also called a *U.S. Savings Bond*. You can buy one for $25. So a bond is only paper that shows that the government owes you money.

As usual, you will get interest back on your money, and there'll be a certain date when you can get the capital and interest back—the maturity date (see chapter 7). The amount of interest you'll get depends on how long you leave your money with the government. Here's the rule: the longer you agree to lend your money, the higher the interest will be.

With Series EE bonds, you must leave the money in for at least six months. These bonds are very safe, so of course interest rates are not as high as those on some other types of lending. As you know, the safer your money is when you lend it, the less interest the borrower must pay you to get you to lend money.

Cities and states

The *municipality* (city or town) and the state in which you live also would like to borrow your money. They also will give you interest, a maturity date, and proof of the loan. This type of borrowing is called *municipal borrowing*, and the proof that you lent the money is called a *municipal bond.*

When you lend money to a municipality, you must be much more careful about its safety than you are with banks or the federal government. Even cities and towns can have money trouble, and if they do, they may not pay you back if things go very badly for them. In Moneytalk, this is called a *default.* Municipal bond defaults are very rare. Still, the possibility worries a lot of people.

To make investing in municipal bonds easier, two companies rate the bonds for safety. Just as you get a grade in school, cities and states get a grade for the safety of their bonds. One company is Standard & Poor's, which grades bonds from AAA to D. The other company is Moody's, which grades bonds from aaa to d (in both cases, the grades work just like yours—the more As the better).

Can you guess which pays more interest to you, a high-grade bond or a low-grade bond? That's right. A low-grade bond pays more interest because the city or state must give you an extra bonus to get you to take the chance on less safety.

Another thing that can happen with a municipal bond is that you may get paid back earlier (but never later) than the maturity date. This is a *call,* in Moneytalk. You don't lose any of your money, but it can make you angry. You get angry for two reasons. First, interest is paid only up to the call date, but you were expecting to be paid up to the date of maturity. Second, now you must find a new place to lend your money, and interest rates may have gone down. In fact, that's probably why a bond is called in the first place. The municipality was able to pay you back fast and borrow new money from others at a lower rate.

Here's an example: Our mom lent money to a municipality in return for a high interest rate. The maturity date, the date she was going to get her money back, was the same year that Arthur would turn eighteen. Our mom wanted to use the money for college. But before Arthur could get to college, the municipality called the bond. It paid our mom back her money with the interest earned—seven years earlier than expected. Our mom had to find a new bond, and interest rates were lower than they were when she'd bought the old bond.

Oh, and one last thing about municipal bonds: When you get interest, there is no tax to pay. The U.S. Constitution doesn't let the federal government tax money paid to you in return for lending your money to a city or state. In chapter 21, you will read a lot about taxes, and you will see that this can be important.

Corporations

Big companies such as Nike, General Motors, Disney, and most others you can think of also want to borrow your money. They give you proof of the loan called a *corporate bond*. The same companies that grade municipal bonds (Standard & Poor's and Moody's) grade corporate bonds. Corporate bonds also have maturity dates and can be called (paid back) early. Some bonds can't be called because they have a *call protection* feature, a promise that they will last until maturity or at least until a specific date.

Lending your money

L ots of businesses and institutions and governments want to borrow your money. But with most of them you must invest at least $1,000, and with some, a lot more. So most of us aren't ready to make that kind of investment. For the future, just remember that no matter whom you lend your money to, the same rules apply.

Always know:

$ **how much interest** you will get

$ **when you will get your money back** (what the maturity date is)

$ **how safe your capital** (money) is

$ **how safe the interest** that your money earns is

Penelope and Sammy shop for interest

S ammy got $25 from his grandfather as a birthday gift. Since he also got lots of toys from his friends, Sammy was willing to put the money in the bank. Penelope also had $25. She saved it from the money her mother gave her to buy games and toys. Penelope and Sammy both went shopping for the best interest rates they could get for lending their money to others.

Einstein and the Rule of 72

The physicist Albert Einstein, one of the most brilliant men who ever lived, discovered the theory of relativity, which is about the way the universe works. But we think he's also important because he said, "Man's greatest invention is compound interest." Why did Einstein say this? Because compound interest adds a lot to your savings.

Compound interest is added to your capital when the interest earned by the capital itself earns interest. The numbers are very impressive. Let's say you start on February 1 with only a penny saved. Let's say you double it every day. So you have two pennies on February 2 and four by February 3. How long do you think it will take to have **$1 million?** Did you say 100 years, 10 years, 1 year? Starting with a penny and doubling every day, you would have over $1 million—$1,316,617.28, to be precise—in only 28 days.

No wonder Einstein was inspired. Of course, we know that your money won't double every day even with compound interest. But at 5 percent compound interest, you will see your $1,000 grow to $2,080 in 15 years; at 10 percent compound interest, the money will double in

Awesome! This is how doubling per day would work:

AMOUNT	DATE	AMOUNT	DATE	AMOUNT	DATE
.01	2/1	10.24	2/11	10,485.76	2/21
.02	2/2	20.48	2/12	20,571.52	2/22
.04	2/3	40.96	2/13	41,143.04	2/23
.08	2/4	81.92	2/14	82,286.08	2/24
.16	2/5	163.84	2/15	164,572.16	2/25
.32	2/6	327.68	2/16	329,154.32	2/26
.64	2/7	655.36	2/17	658,308.64	2/27
1.28	2/8	1,310.72	2/18	1,316,617.28	2/28
2.56	2/9	2,621.44	2/19		
5.12	2/10	5,242.88	2/20		

less than 8 years; and at 20 percent, it will double in less than 4 years.

Here's what Einstein knew: **the rule of 72.** Take the number 72 and divide it by the interest rate you are getting for lending your money. The result is the number of years it will take your money to double.

For example, if you are earning 9 percent interest, divide 72 by 9. The result, 8, is the number of years it will take to double your money. How many years will it take at 8 percent? Right: 9 years (72 ÷ 8 = 9).

They discovered that if they were willing to put money away for a long time and not use it, they would have quite a bit by the time they were ready for college. They also discovered that the interest rate would be 4 percent. They would get this by buying a $25 savings bond from the U.S. government. To buy the bond, they would give the government $17.50 now. In ten years, earning 4 percent interest, the government would return $25 to each of them.

Penelope and Sammy both knew that they were really *lending* their money to the government in return for the interest they would earn. But the banker called it *buying a bond.*

The banker also told them that they could open up a bank account instead. If they did, they would get less interest—only 2 1/2 percent at that moment. This 2 1/2 percent interest would earn them 63 cents per year for their $25 deposit. But each could get his or her money out at any time, without waiting for a maturity date.

It was hard to decide whether to lend their money to the bank or to the government. Finally, Sammy decided to lend his money to the U.S. government for a long time at a higher rate of interest. He did this because his goal was college, and saving for college was part of his plan. Penelope opted for the lower rate and the right to take her money at any time. "After all," she thought, "what if I need to buy something in a hurry and can't wait?"

Would you choose not making much interest but being able to take your money out anytime? Or would you like to have a better chance of making more money but not for a while? Why? How does your answer fit into your goals and plans?

$

Making money

Buying things today that you can sell for more money tomorrow

Another way you can make more money with your money is to invest for *growth*. That means you buy something that becomes more valuable after a while. When it is worth more, you can sell it for more than you paid—that is, you can make a profit (which we discussed in chapter 6).

One example of a growth investment is stocks. *Stocks* are shares in a company. You can buy shares in lots of companies that you know, like PepsiCo or Coca-Cola. If you buy one share of stock in a company that has fifty shares, you actually own one-fiftieth of the company. In fact, most of the companies that want to borrow your money will sell you stock as well. You already know that if you lend money, you make money by getting interest in return for your loan. But if you invest for profit, there are no guarantees. You can make a lot more money than you could as a lender, but you can also lose all or some of your capital (which we discussed in chapter 6).

How to pick the right stocks to make money

When we talked about investing through lending, we worried about safety. And we solved our problem by looking at ratings and guarantees. Now, when we look at investing for profit, we worry about *risk*, which is Moneytalk for how likely you are to lose your money because what you buy (for example, a stock) goes down in value instead of up. We solve our problem by looking at how well the company is doing as a business. It's not hard for you to know which companies make a profit. Kids are some of the best stock pickers around. Just ask yourself and your friends these questions:

$ After school, what **soda and snacks** do you buy?

$ What **video games** do you like best?

$ What **sneakers** do you wear?

§ What **clothing stores** at the mall do you shop in?

§ What **breakfast cereal** do you eat?

When you hear of a company that a lot of kids like, you can do some research to find out if it is a moneymaker. Here's how:

§ Write to the company or visit the company's Web site, and ask for its **annual report.** This tells you how much the company earned last year. Compare the earnings to profits in prior years to see if the company is getting stronger. Every company that offers stock has a Web page dedicated to "stockholder information." You can go there and learn a lot about a company.

§ Find out whether the company has paid out a portion of the money it made to the stockholders. That is called paying a **dividend.** If so, you will receive money even before you sell at a profit.

§ Divide the last dividend paid by the company by the number of shares in the company. This is called the **yield,** in Moneytalk. Compare the yield with those of other stocks. If the yield is higher, the stock is doing well.

For kids who really love stocks

If you really want to make stock picking a hobby and know more about the stock market, one way is to learn about buying stocks before they are popular with everyone else. Then you can sell them at a profit when the market is hot.

The way to do this is with a number called the *P/E,* which stands for *price/earnings ratio.* Every stock has one. The P/E tracks what other people will pay for a stock. *The trick is to buy a stock when the P/E is low, when no one wants it, and then sell when the P/E is high, when everyone will pay a high price.*

To find the P/E, divide last year's earnings per share into the price of the stock today. So if a stock costs $100 per share and earned $10, the P/E is 10 (100 divided by 10 is 10). A P/E of 10 means that investors were willing to pay ten times the earnings for the stock. If the P/E is high, lots of investors want it, and it will cost a lot to buy. If the P/E is low, fewer investors are interested and it goes for a lower price.

A good rule of thumb is to use 12 as an average P/E. Today many stocks are expensive, some with incredibly high P/E ratios. When this happens, it is thought that the market prices will eventually drop to lower the P/E, so many people wait before they buy stocks.

A market of high P/E stocks means people think the stocks will be worth even more later. This is called a *bull market.* When P/Es are low, people think stocks will go down. This is called a *bear market.*

So for kids who love to make money with stocks, try this: without really investing any actual money, pick and follow stocks in your local newspaper, in the *Wall Street Journal,* or online. Lots of colleges already give pretend accounts to kids who participate in investing contests. A few high schools are starting to do the same. But even if there is no organized contest at your school, you can have one right at home by visiting www.betterinvesting.org and going to that site's "Youth Investing" page. You can join a club there or start your own and compare your results with those of your parents, brothers and sisters, or friends. It's cool to see who made more money after three months, and you will learn a whole lot more if you check out the same stocks after six months and after a year.

If you do that, you really see how prices and your money go up and down. You also see that it's just as important to know when to sell as it is to choose a winning stock in the first place. In order to play this stock-picking game, you will have to know how to read the financial pages. You can also find the P/E fast from those pages once you know how to read them.

How to read the financial pages

When you own a stock, you must find out how it is doing. You can do this by reading the financial pages in a newspaper such as the *Wall Street Journal* every day. This is not an easy thing to do at first. But once you get the hang of it, it will become easier. Turn the page to see what a stock report looks like in the paper.

| 52-Week | | | | Yld | | Sales | | | | |
High	Low	Stock	Div	%	P/E	100's	High	Low	Last		Chg
40.37	22.38	MDU	.92 f	3.6	11	810	25.88	25.26	25.33	-	0.29
13.25	1.05	MEMC	...	...	Dd	660	2.31	2.02	2.24	+	0.03
9.4	7.65	MCR	.60	7.2	Q	513	8.44	8.37	8.38	-	0.01
6.82	6.13	MGF	.40	6.0	Q	923	6.75	6.63	6.68	+	0.01
7.01	6.19	MIN	.44	6.5	Q	1617	6.79	6.71	6.75	+	0.03
6.77	5.41	MMT	.47	7.9	Q	631	6.02	5.93	5.94	-	0.07
8.53	7.00	MFM	.53	6.7	Q	356	8.01	7.92	7.92	-	0.05

Let's look at how to read a stock report by using the following example.

1	2	3	4	5	6	7	8	9	10		11
52-Week				Yld		Sales				
High	Low	Stock	Div	%	P/E	100's	High	Low	Last		Chg
12.43	7.00	Innkeepr	1.20	13.1	9	1145	9.40	8.95	9.17	-	0.07
34.10	22.25	Innogy	1.19i	4.1	...	15	29.20	28.90	28.90	-	0.35
14.25	7.38	InputOut	...	...	dd	1102	8.55	8.12	8.37	-	0.28
13.60	9.25	InsigFn	...	...	dd	95	10.00	9.94	9.99		...
4.25	0.65	Insteel	...	...	dd	310	0.93	0.75	0.75	-	0.05
13.74	12.19	InsMuni	.72	5.3	q	152	13.52	13.47	13.52	-	0.08
10.00	4.60	IntegES	...	...	6	270	5.47	5.33	5.38	+	0.05
26.68	14.81	IntAlu	1.20	5.4	21	102	22.70	22.35	22.40		...
119.90	80.06	IBM	.56	0.5	22	101745	102.76	99.85	102.00	+	1.16
31.30	14.69	IntFlav	.60	2.2	31	3254	27.16	26.50	26.80	-	0.22
66.04	33.19	IntGame	...	...	19	7113	49.15	48.48	49.08	-	0.32
23.31	15.94	IntMult	.20j	...	19	466	16.90	15.89	16.25	-	0.23
43.31	26.31	IntPap	1.00	1.00	dd	18304	37.74	37.22	37.70	-	0.20

Look at the numbers across the top of the chart. They are the numbers of the paragraphs that explain each column. Here they are:

1. High for the Year: The first column shows you the highest price per share your stock has been in the past fifty-two weeks.

2. Low for the Year: The second column shows you the lowest price per share your stock has been in the past fifty-two weeks.

3. Stock: The third column tells you which stock this chart refers to.

4. Dividends: A dividend, as we said earlier, is a share of a company's profit that stockholders get. The figure in the paper shows the dividend per share for the current year. Some companies don't pay dividends at all. Some companies may have a dividend one year and not another.

5. % Yield: Divide the dividend by the closing price to get the yield (which we talked about earlier). Remember that you want a high yield.

6. P/E Ratio (price/earnings ratio): As we've explained, the P/E ratio shows how much other investors are willing to pay for a stock. It tells you whether the stock is a bargain or is overvalued. By dividing the earnings into the price, we find out how many times the earnings of a company other investors are willing to pay per share. If they will pay many times earnings, the stock may be too risky, because if they change their mind, you won't be able to sell it for much more than you paid or will even have to sell for less.

7. Sales: This is the number of shares of the company's stock bought and sold (traded) in a day, in hundredths. So 101,745 would be 10,174,500 shares.

8. High: This is how high the price of the stock went that day.

9. Low: This is how low the price of the stock went that day.

10. Last: This is the last price of the stock that day **(closing price).**

11. Change: This shows whether your stock went up or down that day compared to what the last price was at the close on the day before. A plus sign means it went up, and a minus sign means it went down. In this case, $1.16 was the difference.

Using the Internet to pick and follow stocks

The same information in the stock pages can be found on the Internet. In fact, on many Web sites you can get live, up-to-the-minute information, including the price of the stock, the number of shares sold during the trading day, and the latest company news.

The most important asset you have in the investing world isn't the amount of money you have but the amount of information available for your use. Information can lead you to make good investment decisions and avoid bad ones. The Internet is a very powerful tool, one that can help you make good choices with your money.

For example, you can visit www.money.com and learn everything there is to know about a company that you might be thinking of investing in. You can also get information about the overall economy that might help you decide when and where to invest.

MAKING MONEY

Planet Orange—www.orangekids.com—is an awesome site that helped Rose get the concepts that Arthur explained to her. Rose let Cedric and Amy, the site's characters, show her around Planet Orange and around the strange planet of money and savings. She was able to explore the different kinds of money in Money Land, find her way around the stock market on Investor Island, learn what she should expect when she buys everything she wants at South Spending, and help Ashley save up for her snowboard in the Republic of Savings. Enjoying this site is a great way to learn more about the ways of money.

Also, go to the Money Central Station Web site. Learn about how money is made, where it comes from, and what we do with it. This site, supported by the U.S Treasury, is definitely fun and filled with facts that can help you think about money in new ways. Visit Money Central Station at www.moneyfactory.gov/kids/start.html or click the "Money Central Station" link on http://www.kids.gov/k_money.htm.

The kids.gov site also has some other great links, such as Understanding Taxes for Students. That site, brought to you by the Internal Revenue Service (or IRS, the government agency that collects taxes), shows students around the world of taxes. Most of us know the word *taxation* but not much about it. (We talk about this in chapter 21.) When you explore this site, the facts of taxing become much clearer. Now, before you get started on the Internet, be sure to talk with your parents. In fact, it might be best that whenever you use the Internet for financial research, you do so *with* your parents. Remember, you're younger than eighteen, so you can't do anything without your parents' permission, anyway. In addition to all the good information you learn from the Internet, there are a lot of scams. Your parents will be able to help you tell the difference between places that can help you and those that are just looking to make money off of you.

Arthur and Rose's stock tips

$ **Think of the companies you like,** and ask your friends about their favorites.

$ **Watch the news,** and see if any companies are making major changes that could benefit their business.

$ **Get the annual report** and decide if the company is doing well by looking at the things you find in the report's appendix.

$ **Check the P/E** in the financial pages or on the Internet.

$ **If the P/E is low** (under 10 or 11), it could be a winner.

Things to Do

Join a club. Write to the **National Association of Investors Corporation** (NAIC), P.O. Box 220, Royal Oak, MI 48068, call 877-275-6242, or check out their Web site: www.betterinvesting.org. The NAIC even has a special "Youth Investing" page. You will get information on forming a stock club or joining one in your area.

CHAPTER 10

$

Stocks

How to invest money you save from your allowance

Guess who owns Nike, Disney, Pepsi, Coca-Cola, Reebok, and Nintendo? Me!

Paula

Some people think you need to have a lot of money—even be a millionaire—to invest in stocks. That's not true. There are two ways you can be an investor with as little as $10 (although $25 is even better).

Don't *be* a DRIP: Buy one!

There is a program that most large companies have with the funny name of *DRIP*, which stands for *dividend reinvestment plan.* (Remember *dividend* from chapter 9.) When we discussed picking a good stock, one thing we looked for was whether the company pays out its profits as a dividend.

If it does, this dividend can be used to buy more shares in the company itself. This is called *reinvesting.* First, buy a share in a company. Then tell the company to take your dividends and buy more of its stock for you. You have started a DRIP.

Constant reinvesting buys more of a fraction of a share of stock. This goes on and on. Before you know it, you have quite a few dollars invested in the stock.

Unlike investments where you lend money, investing in stocks for profit has no maturity date. If you ever want to sell your shares, you just call the DRIP and tell them to sell and send you the money. Watch the newspaper or follow your stock on the Internet and sell when the value of the shares goes up from the price you paid. That's how you make the biggest profit. *Buy low and sell high!*

Things to Do

To find out which companies have DRIPs and which will put you in the plan with only a few shares, visit www.dripcentral.com or www.fool.com and go to their "DRIP" page.

Buying one share

There are many ways that you can buy one or a few shares with your allowance so you can be part of a DRIP.

$ Join a National Association of Investors Corporation (NAIC) stock club (see chapter 9, and visit www.betterinvesting.org). Lots of companies, including ones you already know, will let you buy one share if you belong to a club.

$ Write to the company of your choice. Some will sell one share directly. **Even if a share costs more money than you have, the company may sell you a fraction of a share.** Let's say that a share of Disney stock costs $30 and you have saved up $15 after making a budget. Just write to the company and say you'd like to buy as large a fraction of a share as possible with $15. Every major company has an "investor relations" page on its Web site. You can find information on DRIPs and learn how to contact the company there.

$ Ask a broker (someone who helps you buy and sell stock) if he or she can sell you a few shares. Most can—but it can cost extra. (We talk more about brokers in chapter 15.)

Remember, shares go up and down in value every day. So if you can buy when the share costs less, you will get more for your $15. This, in Moneytalk, is called *playing the market*. It takes time, knowledge, and experience. Someday soon, with practice, you will be able to do this. For now, work with your parents and get some experience.

Matching Game: Stock Stuff

Match the definition to the word.

1. Undervalued stock

A. Stock of companies that own real estate and equipment equal to or more than the value of their shares

2. Broker

B. Stocks that don't trade on the stock exchange

3. Price/earnings ratio

C. A person licensed to sell stocks, bonds, and other securities

4. Dividends

D. The amount of profit a company pays out to its stockholders

5. Share

E. An investor who thinks the price of stocks will go up

6. OTC stocks

F. Buying stocks with money you borrow from your broker. The stocks you own are **collateral.**

7. Bull

G. An investor who thinks stocks will go down

8. Bear

H. Shows whether investors are willing to pay a lot or a little for the stock

9. Buying on margin

I. Same as stock

Answers: 1 (A), 2 (C), 3 (H), 4 (D), 5 (I), 6 (B), 7 (E), 8 (G), 9 (F)

$

Totally awesome

Stock investment plan for kids who use mutual funds

There are 4,000 mutual funds to choose from. Cool.

Paul

Another way to invest in stocks with very little money is to buy a share in a mutual fund instead of a company. A *mutual fund* is a pool of a lot of people's money that is used to buy a lot of shares of stock in many different companies. The mutual fund manager makes all the decisions. The manager picks the companies she or he thinks will make a profit, decides when to sell, and even tries to judge which stocks will go up and down in value. Knowing who the manager is can be very important in picking a fund that does well.

In Moneytalk, a share in a mutual fund is called a *unit*. A few mutual funds will sell you a unit for $10, some insist on $25, and others ask for more. But since there are about 4,000 mutual funds in this country, you'll find one in which to invest.

Before you buy, you'll get a booklet called a *prospectus*. Even though you may fall asleep a few times trying to read the important parts (it's not the most thrilling stuff in the world), it's worthwhile to get this information.

The prospectus tells you things like

- $ what a fund invests in
- $ who the manager is
- $ what expenses you pay
- $ what the fund's goals are

Mutual funds help you put your (nest) egg in a lot of baskets by making it easy to diversify. The great thing about a mutual fund is that you get a tiny part of lots of different stocks. This way, you don't have to choose only one company that you like. A mutual fund gives you many different investments. So if one company isn't doing very well, another might be. This cuts your risk. Because we kids don't usually have a lot of money to invest, there is really no other way for us to diversify except in mutual funds.

The All-the-Eggs-in-One-Basket Game

You have 10 eggs that you have just taken from the chicken house. The Fox wants the eggs but can only carry 1 basket. You have 10 baskets. Each basket holds from 1 to 10 eggs. What is the best way to put the eggs in the baskets to make them safe from the Fox?

Well, it's your choice. If you put all the eggs in one basket, you will keep all the eggs 9 out of 10 times. But if the Fox gets a hold of that basket, you'll lose everything. If you put 1 egg in each basket, you may lose 1 to the Fox while you handle all the others. But at least the other 9 would be safe.

This way of protecting what you have is called **diversification.** If you put all your eggs in one basket, you may lose everything one day. If you put 1 egg in each, you'll probably lose at least 1 but not more. A good idea is to handle 3 or 4 baskets—not too many to keep track of, but still enough to leave you a lot of eggs if the Fox steals one.

Dollar cost averaging:
How Any Kid Can Be a Great Investor

There is a special system for people with small amounts of money to invest that gives you the most profit. It can make any kid a great investor, and it's easy to follow. In

Moneytalk, it's called *dollar cost averaging,* or *DCA.* It works best with mutual funds.

All you need is a little extra money for investing every week. A dollar is good enough; more is okay, too.

Next, decide what you want to invest in. You can pick a single stock in a DRIP or a mutual fund. DCA doesn't work with the type of investing that is really lending.

After you pick your mutual fund or DRIP, buy more every week or month. *The trick is to put exactly the same amount into the investment each time.* If you do, a funny thing happens. You end up buying more of the stocks or units at a lower price than at a higher price. If the stock goes up while you're buying, you do well because you have more shares. If it goes down, your risk is limited because you've bought a portion of your shares at a lower price. As you know, the best way to make a profit is to buy low and sell high. With dollar cost averaging, you can buy low, so you are halfway there.

To understand why, you have to do some math and understand how averages work. But with or without the math, the idea is easy. Just save the same amount of money each week, and use it to make an investment in the same stock or mutual fund. By the time you go to sell, you will have paid less for each share or unit than if you'd had lots of money and bought all at once (either at the original high price if the stock went down or at the final high price if the stock went up).

Paula buys a money tree

Paula is eleven years old. She told her parents that she saw a show about how important college is. She wanted to

Things to Do

For a list of mutual funds that charge no commissions (called no-load funds and discussed in chapter 15):

Write to No Load Fund Investor, 410 Sawmill River Road, Suite #2060, Ardsley, NY 10502, call 1-800-252-2042, or check out the Web site www.sheldon-jacobs.com

Or write to Mutual Fund Education Alliance, call 816-454-9422, or check out www.mfea.com.

start saving for it. Her parents gave her $50 to start her college fund. But Paula didn't know how to begin, so she asked her parents what to do. They told her she could choose from stocks, bonds, and mutual funds. She looked at stocks but thought that they were too risky. She didn't like bonds because they didn't make as much money as she wanted.

Then she looked at mutual funds. She saw that they are a group of stocks and that they are a little safer. She looked further into kinds of mutual funds: *growth, income,* and some others. She looked at all of them. She saw that a *growth mutual fund* was for people who could wait for their money for several years. She also saw that *income mutual funds* were best for people who needed money now. She thought that a growth mutual fund would be better for her college fund.

What things would you like to think about before you make an investment decision?

Here's our list:

1. What is my goal or purpose? (For example, do I want to grow my money for the future or buy something I need but don't have the money to get?)

2. Can I afford to make this investment? What's the minimum I need to invest? (For example, would I want to invest $250 in a mutual fund or $1.50 in a baseball card?)

3. In the past, how much money has been made by investments like the one I'm thinking about? during what time period?

4. Can I sell and get my money back anytime I want, or do I have to wait for a maturity date?

5. Are there any guarantees, or could I lose all or part of my money?

6. Who controls or manages the investment? (For example, is there a mutual fund manager?)

7. Do I already have too many investments like this one?

8. What are the fees or costs to make the investment?

Asking and answering these questions can help you make smarter investing decisions, and can make or save you money.

CHAPTER 12

$

Other stuff you can buy to make a profit

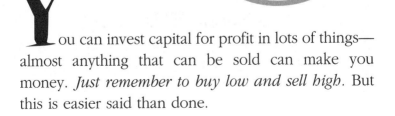

Do I want real estate or collect-ibles? Hmm, I think I'll collect real estate!

Marvin Mogul

You can invest capital for profit in lots of things—almost anything that can be sold can make you money. *Just remember to buy low and sell high*. But this is easier said than done.

Most things that make a profit are too expensive for kids to invest in. So when we thought about them—things like real estate, gold, and oil that grown-ups talk about to make money—we said, "No way!" But then we found out that all these things can also be bought with a unit in a mutual fund. When you get older and have more money, you can buy them with or without a fund. Here are some amazing things that can be invested in through a mutual fund.

Real estate

R*eal estate* is Moneytalk for *property* such as a house and land or a bunch of stores or malls. The majority of Americans own some sort of real estate—in fact, as this is being written, a record number of Americans own their own home.

And even if you can't afford your own home or property, you can invest in real estate through a mutual fund called a *real estate investment trust,* or REIT. If you own shares in a REIT, you own part of some property that is managed for all the REIT's investors. The property is owned by everyone through a trust. In a *trust* one person manages something for the benefit of others. Just as a stock mutual fund owns a lot of stocks, a REIT owns a lot of property.

Commodities

In Moneytalk, *commodities* are "stuff." A commodity can be anything that is bought and sold all the time. Commodities are traded on an exchange just like stocks and mutual funds. Some examples are gold, silver, metals, farm products such as meat and soybeans, and even foreign currency. These investments have the most risk because they have no guarantees like lending does, and they have no reliable performance records like stock in companies does. But many people invest in commodities because they believe the risk is worth the chance to make lots of money.

The price of commodities also affects the price of other things you buy every day. For example, the price of oil has a direct impact on the price of the gas your parents need to fill the tanks of their cars. The price of pork bellies impacts the price of bacon you can buy in the supermarket. In our economy, everything is linked.

Recently we had what some people referred to as an oil crisis, when the price of gasoline went up high. People who owned the commodity of gasoline owned the rights in something very valuable, and they made a lot of money. So mostly you make money in a commodity when there is not much of it and people want it. For instance, if bad weather killed lots of oranges, people would pay a lot for orange juice because it would be hard to get. And people who owned the commodity of oranges would make more money.

Collectibles

A *collectible* is anything you buy and can resell at a profit. Sound familiar? Arthur has a baseball card collection. Do you collect anything? If you do, you are already an investor. If you do collect stuff that you can resell, answer these questions about your collection. They will tell you a lot about the type of investor you are.

$ Do you collect lots of inexpensive things, like postage stamps that are not rare yet, or a few big, expensive things, like special dolls?

$ Do you pay attention to the cost and resale value of the things you collect?

$ Do you keep a record of the cost of your collectibles?

$ Have you ever thought of selling some of the things in your collection for a profit?

$ Do you trade with your friends?

$ Do you know any dealers in your area personally?

To have a successful collection, you must do many things.

1. You must be serious.

2. You must keep good records. For example:

$ When you buy something for your collection, always keep a receipt.

$ Put the receipts in a folder for safekeeping.

$ When you sell, keep a record of the price you got.

3. Keep an inventory of what you have, what it cost, and what it's worth today. You can look up the values of all kinds of collectibles on the Internet by searching around eBay and other Web sites dedicated to your specific kind of collection.

4. Always keep your collection in **mint** (the best) **condition**. Those items will bring you the most money on resale.

5. Don't get caught up in a fad. Rose owns 350 Beanie Babies. They cost about $7 each, new. At one time just one of them was worth $350, but now none of them are worth much. She is selling them all to a dealer for $350—a big loss.

Marvin Mogul and the baseball card sale

Ten-year-old Marvin was a real fan of baseball cards. In fact, his room was cluttered with them. He didn't know how to get rid of them because he didn't want to give them away or throw them away. So he asked his older brother, Tom, what to do. Tom said, "Sell them at a profit, sort of like when there's a garage sale." "Great idea," said Marvin. He gathered most of his cards (he kept some so he wouldn't have to restart his collection entirely). He also bought a magazine that told him the prices of all the baseball cards. He sold some cards when his parents had a lawn sale, and he sold the rest on the Internet with the help of his parents.

Marvin found that keeping good records and making sure that his collection was in good shape made a real difference when it came time to sell. He made more money because his collection was well preserved and catalogued.

Collector's Record

Item Bought	Price Paid	Today's Value (update every six months)	Date Sold	Price Received

Rhonda Realtor
and the Real Estate Deal

Twelve-year-old Rhonda wanted to be a real estate agent when she grew up. That meant she would make money helping other people buy and sell their property. Usually, the seller would pay her a percentage of the sale price of the property. But she would make money only if the sale went through.

To practice for her future, Rhonda decided to help kids sell playhouses they'd built. (Rhonda made an extra profit by selling the plans for these houses.) But she was having trouble selling one of the houses. It cost $40, and nobody wanted to buy it. She didn't know what to do.

She asked her friends what to do, but none of them knew. Then, after two weeks, Rhonda had an idea: maybe she should lower the price. She did, and she sold the house in a week.

What are some things you would do to make a playhouse or anything else sell faster?

Discuss your ideas with your parents.

§

How you can help save the planet

The best part of investing is that it gives you a say in lots of things. In school and at home, you probably learn about things that are very wrong with the world. Sometimes, all this can scare you. Things like global warming, oil spills, and governments that deny human rights can also make you angry. But, hey, you're just a kid, so what can you do about it?

Investing right can help make a better world.

Once you become an investor, you can do plenty. Any stockowner, even one with only one share, can go to a stockholders' meeting. Most of the time, the meetings are held once a year. At the meeting, anyone can speak up about the company. If it pollutes the environment or does anything else you don't like, you can say so. If you can't get to the meeting, you can write.

But more powerful than speaking up at meetings is choosing to invest in companies that don't do the things you are against and that try to do the things you are for. There are companies, for instance, that make a special effort to clean up the environment, don't do business with countries that deny civil rights, and treat women and minorities fairly. In Moneytalk, investing in these companies is called *socially responsible investing*. Too bad all companies aren't socially responsible. When you grow up, maybe you can help make more companies be that way.

Today, some areas of socially responsible investing are companies that work on forestation, water resources, safer and cheaper energy, better waste disposal, and control of noise and other kinds of pollution. Asian and European companies are growing fastest in these areas.

Things to Do

If you like the idea of making money in a socially responsible way, you can do it with our old friend the mutual fund. Here are the names of a few:

$ Global Environment Fund, www.globalenviron-mentfund.com, 202-789-4500

$ Domini Social Index Trust, www.domini.com, 1-800-762-6814

$ Calvert Social Investment Fund, www.calvert.com, 1-800-368-2748

$ Pax World Fund, www.paxworld.com, 1-800-767-1729

$ You can learn more about a variety of socially responsible investing opportunities by visiting www.socialinvest.org, the Web site of the Social Investment Forum.

It's important to know that investing in a socially responsible company doesn't mean you'll make more money. Sometimes, companies that do things you don't like make the most money. One of the toughest decisions for an investor to make is whether to try to make money or to make a little less with a socially responsible attitude.

Here's what Rose does when she reads the boring prospectus for any mutual fund or company. If the fund does well and also does good things for the environment, that's one she'll choose. If a fund or company makes a lot of money and she reads in the papers that it did a bad thing, she won't invest in it, even if she could make a profit. If a company is neutral, she'll invest in that, too. Every kid must make his or her own decisions. How do you feel about these issues?

Gerald invests in his future

Ten-year-old Gerald had just received $25 from his parents as a Christmas gift. He decided to invest it. But he didn't know how to do this, so he went to the magazine store and bought a copy of the *Wall Street Journal*.

Around this same time, he saw a TV show about the environment, which he wanted to help save. He wanted to invest in companies that he believed were doing the right thing about the environment. He also wanted to find companies that were hiring men and women equally. He found a new company that was researching cheaper ways to recycle paper. It was $1 a share, so Gerald bought 25 shares.

What do you want your perfect company to be like?

$

Where in the world is your money?

Kids' money can make money from investments in many parts of the world. With the awesome technology we have, all of us will one day be invested in almost every country in the world and have stocks in foreign companies. Imagine yourself lending money to France or Korea!

In Moneytalk, this is called *global investing*. You can start right now to be a global investor. Here's how.

International mutual funds

R emember the mutual fund? Buying a unit in a mutual fund gives you a small share in the hundreds of investments owned by the fund. The cool thing is that these foreign investments can be in almost anything that makes a profit: stocks, real estate, gold, even money lent to foreign governments. If you buy a *global* or *international mutual fund,* you own a piece of lots of foreign companies.

There are even funds that concentrate on one country at a time, like the Spain and the Philippines Funds. Right now, some countries, like Mexico and Brazil, are "hot." They are called *emerging growth countries,* in Moneytalk. Some people believe that these will become big-profit countries. But such changes are hard to predict, so these are risky. Other countries, like most of those in Europe, have been doing business for a long time and are safer, but they may not give you as much profit. You always have to balance the risk and the reward—especially in global investing.

Other ways to make a profit in foreign countries

M utual funds are not the only way to invest in foreign stocks. Many foreign companies sell stock through U.S. brokers, professionals who are licensed to sell stock (as we mentioned in chapter 10). You'll find out how to buy stock from them in chapter 15.

Some companies don't sell stock through U.S. brokers or mutual funds. But you can invest in them by buying *American Depository Receipts,* or *ADRs.* These are proof that you've bought a foreign stock, and the proof is held in a bank outside the United States. As kids, we probably will never buy an ADR. But it's good to know they exist, because when we grow up, we will be more likely to invest in foreign companies than our parents and grandparents have been. The world is growing smaller, and investment choices are available in every country. This is why we now talk about the *global economy.* By the time you are grown up, we will have less resistance to investing around the world. Also, we might win the lottery, travel abroad, and get interested in a foreign company. Hey, you never know!

Lending money to royalty

Another way to make money globally is to lend money to foreign governments and companies. This is just like buying U.S. government and corporate bonds, which you read about in chapter 8. All the same rules apply:

- $ You know the safety of capital and interest.
- $ You know when you can get your money back.
- $ You know the interest you will get.

And guess what? There are mutual funds that own only foreign corporate and government bonds. They are called *foreign income funds.* Some of the countries in these funds are run by kings and queens, so investing this way can be like lending your money to royalty.

Currency: The most fun to have with money

Maybe you are wondering how buying foreign money makes money. We learned about it on a trip we took to England with our parents. We noticed that our mom had U.S. dollars but that all the prices were in English pounds (that's what paper money is called in England).

Since the stores, hotels, and restaurants didn't accept dollars, we had to change them (*convert,* in Moneytalk) into pounds. The tricky part was that one dollar did not equal one pound. And what was more confusing, the amount of dollars a pound did equal changed every day. One day a pound cost $1.80; another day it cost $1.85. Of course, the fewer dollars my mother paid for the pounds, the happier she was. This was getting interesting.

At the end of the trip, our mom had lots of pounds left, so she had to convert those back into dollars. On the day we left for home, the pound equaled $1.83. That meant our mom made 3 cents for every pound she converted that she'd bought at $1.80 and lost 2 cents on every pound she'd bought at $1.85.

That's how I learned that you can make and lose money on *currency conversion,* or *exchange.* It's another way to invest that's risky, but it sure is a lot of fun.

The main thing to remember is that every time you make any kind of global investment, you are also investing in the currency involved in the investment.

This is especially true if you are lending your money to a

foreign government or company and getting a bond back. At the maturity date, you will get your money back in foreign currency. When you convert it to dollars, you may make or lose money on the exchange.

The world of money changes, just like all other parts of our world. It used to be that countries in Europe had different currencies. In France it was the franc, in Germany it was the mark. Then some European countries decided to get one common currency called the euro, which is what they have today.

The World of Money Game

Unscramble the unit of currency in column A and then match it with the place it is spent in column B.

Column A	Column B
1. darn	**a.** India
2. ad roll	**b.** Most of Europe
3. pose	**c.** Russia
4. reuo	**d.** Canada
5. noupd	**e.** Mexico
6. puree	**f.** Japan
7. luber	**g.** England
8. eny	**h.** South Africa

Answers: 1. rand (h) 2. dollar (d) 3. peso (e) 4. euro (b) 5. pound (g) 6. rupee (a) 7. ruble (c) 8. yen (f)

$

Bankers, brokers, financial planners, and other money experts

---

There are many types of professionals who can help you handle your money. They have different educational backgrounds, do different things, have different titles, and work in different kinds of places. We spoke to a lot of them while writing this book, and we can tell you one thing: they all like to talk to kids. Don't ever be afraid to ask them questions. Giving helpful answers is a big part of their jobs. Here is who they are and what they can do for you.

Bankers

Banker is a word for many kinds of people who work in a bank. The one you'll probably meet first is the *teller.* That person takes your money and puts it into your savings or checking account.

Another type of banker is a *loan officer.* He or she sees whether the bank is willing to lend you money. (You'll read all about loan officers in chapter 16.)

A third type of banker is the *bank manager.* This person makes sure the bank is running smoothly and handles your complaints.

Finally, there is the *president* of the bank and the people on the *board of directors.* As you know, banks borrow your money and use it to invest for profit. These bankers, among other things, decide how the bank's money will be invested.

Brokers

A s we first mentioned in chapter 10, *brokers* are people who have taken and passed a special exam that allows them to buy and sell stocks and bonds. Without this license, they can't make trades for you. Brokers study different types of investments and make suggestions about what you should buy. You can make your own choices or follow your broker's advice. Most investors do a little bit of both.

Stocks are traded through *stock exchanges* that are under heavy government regulation. It's very important that people like us who buy and sell stock do so in a fair market. So the stock salespeople or brokers must be licensed.

Brokers get paid every time you buy or sell a stock or bond. Sometimes they get a percentage of the purchase or sale price. This is called a *commission* in Moneytalk and is usually how the broker gets paid when you buy and sell stock.

Sometimes brokers get a *markup* instead of a commission. A markup is Moneytalk for the difference between what the broker pays for the item and the price at which he or she sells it to you. A markup is usually the way the broker gets paid for buying bonds for you.

Guess who pays the broker the commission or markup? You!

That's why many people like to use special brokers called *discount brokers.* They charge a set price, depending on the size of your investment, which is lower than what most other brokers charge. But many times they don't give you advice; they just make trades.

To kids, the commission a broker gets is very important because we don't always have a lot to invest. Sometimes, the broker's fee can be more than our investment! For example, some companies charge a minimum of $37 to buy or sell stock.

Also, brokers' fees are lowest if an investor buys at least 100 shares of a stock. This is called a *round lot*, in Moneytalk. Most kids can buy only a couple of shares. A sale of less than 100 is called an *odd lot*. So even if we didn't buy much, we'd end up paying more in commission.

That's why we like DRIPs, which are discussed in chapter 10. There is no commission at all. Also, some mutual funds can be bought without a commission. They are called *no-load funds*, in Moneytalk. Still, it's better to have a good investment that costs a commission than a bad one without a commission.

There are also a number of companies that do not use brokers but that place trades electronically, using the Internet. One such company can be found at www.sharebuilder.com, which charges as little as $4 per trade. But be careful—some of these companies charge you monthly fees in addition to commissions. You should look around the Internet with your parents if you want to trade online.

Financial planners: New kids on the block

Financial planners are people who help you decide which investments are best for you. They look at your income, your expenses, and the amount of risk you want to take. They also look at your goals and when you want to achieve them. With all this information, they make a special plan for you to follow.

Financial planners are not licensed, but a lot of them are *certified financial planners,* or *CFPs.* To be certified, they must take special courses and pass examinations.

Sometimes financial planners are also brokers. If so, they also get a markup or commission if you buy what they suggest. Sometimes they are paid for their time by the hour. The average financial plan takes about twenty hours to complete and is hard work, so getting one can be expensive. Because of this, most planners make money through commissions.

Real estate agents

A *real estate agent,* or *broker,* helps you find and buy property. This could include a house, land, or stores you wanted to rent or buy. They get a commission, usually around 6 percent of the sale price or two months' rent.

Insurance agents

I *nsurance agents* sell you life, health, auto, and home insurance. The different types of insurance are a way of reducing your money worries if something goes wrong. You pay an insurance company a little bit of money every month and if something bad happens, the insurance company pays to help fix it. They will pay auto mechanics, carpenters, and more, depending on what kind of insurance you buy.

Lawyers, accountants, and CPAs

There are many other professionals who may help you with your money. *Lawyers* and *accountants* can help prepare your taxes, give you business advice, and negotiate deals for you.

Some accountants take a special exam that certifies them. They are called *certified public accountants,* or *CPAs.* They can help you with your taxes and also act for you in front of the IRS, which you'll read more about in chapter 21.

Match the Professionals Game

Match the professionals with the things they do for you:

1. Buying home insurance

2. Making a financial portfolio

3. Granting a loan

4. Selling a house

5. Buying auto insurance

6. Buying stock

7. Doing your taxes

8. Closing on property

a. Financial planner

b. Banker

c. Real estate agent

d. Insurance agent

e. Stockbroker

f. Lawyer

g. Insurance salesman

h. Accountant

Answers: a (2), b (3), c (4), d (1), e (6), f (8), g (5), h (7)

Read this before you buy from a broker

$ **A regular broker** charges you a percentage of the price of the stocks and bonds you buy or sell. So if you buy $2,000 worth of stock, it might cost you $70.

$ **A discount broker** charges you a smaller percentage of the price. So a $2,000 buy could cost only $40.

$ **A deep-discount broker** charges you on the number of shares you buy, not on the amount you invest. This can be much cheaper if you make a big purchase or sale. But this kind of broker usually charges a minimum of about $37, so we small investors don't save much.

$ **DRIPs** avoid brokers altogether because you buy directly from the company, at no cost. This is a great idea for kids, but not all companies offer this option.

Here's what we do about brokers: Even though it costs a little more, we have one regular broker to give us advice, do research, and direct us toward good investment choices. We also have one discount broker when we know just what we want and don't need to talk to anyone. We buy through DRIPs whenever possible.

Credit & debt: Two sides of the same coin

Credit card

Responsibility to pay back with interest

Candy Creditworthy

Don't take one if you don't want the other.

Sometimes you can't save enough money to get what you want. When that happens, there may be someone who is willing to let you use his or her money, as long as you pay that lender back with interest. If you've read chapter 8 on investing, you already know that banks, corporations, and governments offer you interest in order to use your money. Well, you must do the same in order to borrow money from them or from anyone else.

In Moneytalk, when you use someone else's money to get something you want, it's called *borrowing*. As a borrower, you must pay back the money with extra money called *interest*. If you are the one letting others use your money, it's called *lending*. You are the lender, and you get your money back someday with interest.

The ability to borrow money is called *credit*, in Moneytalk. Everyone wants credit in case they need to buy something they can't afford right away. But here's the catch: once you use the credit, you must pay back the money. This responsibility to pay back is called *debt*. No one likes to be in debt, even though most Americans are.

▬ ▬ ▬ ▬ ▬ ▬ ▬ ▬

The Marble-Borrowing Game

In order to play in a marbles tournament, you need 100 marbles. Pretend you have only 50 and need 50 more. What can you do? You can promise to pay 10 marbles a day for six days to someone if he or she lets you borrow the marbles. This will pay back the player who lends you the marbles (60 all together—50 for what was lent, plus 10 as interest). But you'd better win the tournament, or you won't have any marbles to pay back.

This isn't much of a game. But by the time you owe so much, you've probably lost your marbles!

▬ ▬ ▬ ▬ ▬ ▬ ▬ ▬

How expensive is money to borrow?

All the things you wanted to know when you invest by lending (see chapter 7) are the things a lender wants to know when you borrow money from him or her. How sure are they that you will pay them back? A person who has borrowed money before and has a good record of paying back is a good choice for a lender. Willingness of a lender to trust you is called your *creditworthiness,* in Moneytalk. The amount they are willing to lend to you is called your *line of credit.*

If you have a record of failure to pay, your creditworthiness is low, and you may not be able to get a line of credit. To borrow money, you would have to pay a lot more interest to get the lender to take the risk that you'd pay them on a new loan. Also, the lender will ask certain questions:

$ How long do you want to keep the money?

Most of the time, the longer you want to keep the money, the lower the interest rate. Short-term borrowing is more expensive. This always sounds funny to me, but there is a reason it's true. Lenders have to work hard to check out your creditworthiness. Once they are satisfied that they can trust you, they want you to keep their money and pay them interest every year. If you pay them off fast, they have to find someone else to lend to. That's extra work. So lenders will charge a creditworthy person less interest if he or she sticks with the loan for a long time.

$ How much do you want to borrow?

Maybe you can guess that usually the more you borrow, the lower the interest is. That's for the same reason we just saw. The lender has to work hard only once to find a borrower who wants to borrow a lot of money. It's easier than finding many small borrowers.

So it actually costs less to borrow a lot than a little. Unfortunately, most people don't get the interest rate break. Borrowers like corporations borrow so much that they get a discount on the interest rate. This is called **prime rate,** in Moneytalk. It's a cheaper way of borrowing than individuals ever get. Bummer! Still, the rates we are charged for borrowing are usually based on a few percentage points more than the prime rate. This means that when the interest rate for big-business borrowing goes down, it usually goes down for us, too.

$ Will you give them anything you already own that they can keep if you don't pay them back?

If you give lenders something valuable they can keep, they feel better about lending. If you don't pay—or **default,** in Moneytalk (as mentioned in chapter 8)—they keep the item, sell it, and get their money anyway. So if you have something valuable to put up for a loan (called **collateral,** in Moneytalk) you can borrow money more cheaply than if you don't. Can you guess the two main things that grown-ups put up as collateral? **That's right: their house and their car.**

Your credit rating: One number that can make you a lot of money

Remember the term *creditworthiness* you just read about? Well, your creditworthiness is tracked using a formula that produces a number called your *credit score.* This score, which is on a scale of 375 to 900, tells lenders a lot about the person who wants their money. All the information that lenders look for (your record of paying back money, how much you've borrowed in the past, etc.) is put into the formula, along with a report that includes information on all of your borrowing transactions.

Your credit score is one of the main factors that determine whether lenders will lend you money and what interest rate they will charge. The higher your score, the more likely lenders are to trust you, and the lower the interest rate they will expect in return for their money.

So remember, every time you get a credit card, forget to pay a bill, or take out a loan, it will be reflected on your report. You can build good credit by paying your bills on time and paying your credit cards back on schedule.

You can access your credit report online for free by visiting www.annualcreditreport.com. In fact, the federal government recently passed a law that allows you to access the report once a year from each of the three companies that maintain credit reports. Once you look at your report, be sure to check that it is accurate. Often, mistakes are made, and it is up to you to correct them. You can do that by writing to the credit bureau and following the instructions on the Web site. Make sure your report is accurate! Mistakes can cost you a lot of money!

How to shop for money

You can see that money can be borrowed expensively or cheaply. If you need to borrow, you want the interest to be as low as possible. You can shop around for money just the way you do for toys and games.

Shopping for money is called *comparing interest rates,* in Moneytalk. Here is how it works:

Let's say you want to borrow $10. The lender will say, "Our interest rate is 5 percent." (No matter how much you need to borrow, the cost is always expressed in a percentage.) Of course, 5 percent of $10 is 50 cents. So when you pay back the money, the lender gets $10.50.

Let's say you used the money to buy clothes. The storekeeper sells you $10 worth of clothes, but you have to pay the lender $10.50. That's why things bought with borrowed money are always more expensive than things bought with saved money. You end up having to work harder and save longer to pay the lender than to buy the thing itself.

Here are some of the places where you can go to borrow money:

$ Some stores will lend you money to buy their stuff by issuing you store credit.

$ Credit card companies will give you a borrowing card.

$ Banks will give you loans with and without collateral.

You shop for credit by comparing the interest rates they charge. Let's look at some real-life examples.

The plastic flash: Credit cards

A *credit card* is a plastic card that allows you to buy stuff without paying for it right away. The companies, such as American Express, VISA, MasterCard, Discover Card, and many others, lend you money to buy the items you want.

Credit card loans are easy to get, but the interest rate is high. You probably already know why the cost of using a credit card is higher than the cost of other credit:

- **$** There is no collateral.
- **$** The loan is small.
- **$** It's for a short period of time.

If you don't repay the amount you've borrowed every month exactly on time, you get charged an interest rate of up to 20 percent. This means that what you bought costs 20 percent more than it would have if you'd paid with a check or cash.

Spend-and-save cards

Today, there is a new choice called *spend-and-save cards*. For every dollar you spend, you get a refund or another type of bonus at the store where you made the purchase. We can't decide about whether these cards a good idea. Of course, it's nice to get money back if you are going to buy something. But having one also may convince you to buy something you don't need, like a sale does sometimes. For now, our advice is to use the spend-and-save card if you're going to buy the item anyway but to avoid getting sucked into buying things you don't really want just because you get a small bonus.

How do you feel about credit cards? Our view is that using credit cards is fine if you're buying things that will last a long time. Also, they're convenient, and allow you to keep good records because of the monthly statements (or lists of purchases) you receive from the credit card company.

As you can see, sometimes credit is good to use, but it can also get you into trouble. Being able to spend smartly is very important to your financial well-being.

Borrowing and a kid's future

Credit is like a tool that helps you build fast.

When borrowing is no good

Reports say that the U.S. government is in so much debt that we, today's kids, will have to pay for it all our lives. This means that when we pay our taxes, which you'll read

But...if you use too much credit, it can destroy all you have.

about in chapter 21, a lot of the money will go to pay for things the government bought a long time ago, instead of for new things that we need. An example is roads and bridges. By the time we need new ones, our tax dollars may be going to pay the debt on old ones built years ago.

Even worse, people and governments sometimes spend money wastefully on silly things. This situation becomes very bad when they have to borrow in order to replace the money they've wasted. It means that for years they must pay back money used for things that did them no good in the first place.

So we can pretty much agree that using *credit* (see chapter 16) is no good when:

- 💲 **the interest rates are high,** and the money is expensive to get

- 💲 **the thing you buy with it disappears fast,** and the only thing left is the debt you have to pay back

- 💲 **you don't have enough income** to make the payments, and you have to default (not pay)

When you don't pay, you can lose your collateral or get sued. Worst of all, you'll end up with a bad credit rating. This means that the next time you ask to borrow, the lender will charge you more money in interest to make up for your bad creditworthiness.

But sometimes borrowing money can work well and get you just what you want. In fact, borrowing money can be just what you need to be a success.

Totally awesome ways of borrowing money

By borrowing money, you can buy and own investments much faster than if you saved up from your income. When you use the very thing that you are buying as collateral for the loan you are taking to buy it, this is called *leverage,* in Moneytalk. Leverage allows you to increase your success as an investor. For example, when you get older and are investing in stocks, you can open a special account that allows you to borrow money from the brokerage firms to buy stocks. You can borrow up to 50 percent of the value of the stocks you have in your stock account. In Moneytalk, this is called *buying on margin.*

Buying a house

The best example of how leverage works is buying a house. If your parents own their own home, they probably used leverage to buy it. If they did, that was a good type of borrowing, not a bad one. Here's how it works:

Let's say your mom and dad have $40,000 to buy a house. Maybe they saved it by making a budget. Perhaps it took five years to save all that money. Let's say they decide that your family needs more room or a neighborhood with a good school.

So now they go shopping for a house. Wow! Prices are high. The house they like costs $180,000. If it took them five years to save $40,000, it could take them another fifteen to twenty years to save the rest.

They decide to borrow $140,000 to pay for the house and buy it right away. Luckily, a bank, the seller of the house, or another lender agrees to loan them the money if they'll put up the house they will buy as collateral.

In other words, if your parents default, the lender can take the house back. But if they finish paying the loan, they'll own the house outright when they've made the last payment. The right of the lender to take the house back if payment is not made is on record in the county clerk's office where you live. The paper that gets recorded is called a *mortgage,* in Moneytalk.

This is a totally cool way of borrowing money. Look at all the good it does:

$ Your mom and dad get to buy a house years earlier than they could by saving.

$ You get to live in it and enjoy it.

$ Eventually, they pay off the mortgage, and they own the house with no debt.

$ Believe it or not, the government gives them a tax break for taking the loan. (You'll read about that in chapter 21.)

How leverage makes you money

Here's why leverage is more than cool—it's awesome! Let's say your mom and dad decide to sell the house before they pay off the mortgage. Maybe they've found a house they like better, or one of them wants to move to get a better job. Even though they've used the house as collateral, they can still sell it.

Let's say it is now worth $200,000. The price went up because of the nice things your folks did to fix it up. It's worth more now than when they bought it. All they have to pay back is the amount they borrowed. They can pay that from the sale price of the house. Guess what! They get to keep the extra $60,000 as a profit. That's a pretty good investment.

Leverage for math brains

Here's something for math brains. If your folks paid the whole $180,000 and did not take a loan but used cash, how much of a percentage did they make on their investment if they sold for $200,000? Answer: 11.11 percent. (The profit of $20,000 is 11.11 percent of $180,000.)

Since your folks did borrow and put only $40,000 into the

house, how much of a percentage did they make if they sold the house at the same $200,000? Answer: 50 percent. The profit of $20,000 ($200,000 - $180,000) is 50 percent of $40,000—minus whatever interest they had to pay on the loan.

In the first case, they made an 11.1 percent profit. Cool! In the second case, they made a 50 percent profit, turning $40,000 into $60,000!

You can use leverage to buy lots of things: a business, a stock, artwork. But remember, try to pick something that will have the same or higher value in the future, or you can be left with a debt instead of a profit.

The Leverage Game

Each player begins at Start. The first player chooses from one to four dice to throw at each turn. For every die the players choose, they are down 5 points. But they get to move the number of spaces that the total throw gives them. They then win or lose the points indicated on the space in which they landed.

So a player can leverage his or her turn (that is, increase its power) by using more dice. Naturally, with leverage, the player also takes the extra risk of throwing less than a 5 with any of the dice chosen. Since each die "costs" 5 points to use, it's important that the return be a 5 or more to help the player win.

In real investing, leverage also helps you make money faster, so in our game, there are extra points for the player who comes in first, no matter what his or her point total is by the end of the game. The first to end the game wins 100 points; the second, 75 points; the third, 50 points.

Play the game five times, and the one with the most game and speed points wins.

What kind of player are you? Do you like to take the risk and leverage your turn, or do you play it slow and safe?

+10	+10	+10		-10	+15	+15
-5		-10		+10		-15
-5		-10		+10		-20
+5		+10		-10		-5
+5		+5		+5		+5
+5		+5		+5		+10
+5		+5		+5		+15
+5		-5		-5		+20
+5		-5		-10		0
START		+10	+10	-10		END

PART 4

Money and real life

> Do what you love. The money will follow.*
>
> Irwin Earner

*Title of a great book by Marsha Sinetar

Of course, all money matters have to do with real life. But there are some things that we have to do almost every day that relate to money. One of them is to work and get paid. It's no fun to pick a job just to make

136

money. When you grow up, we hope you pick work you love to do.

But most kids work just to get paid. They need some extra money, so they deliver groceries or have a paper route. Arthur liked the idea of being in business, but Rose has been babysitting and doing other odd jobs for extra money.

Whatever way you make money, you have to know what to charge and make sure you get paid. It's not easy when the people who give you the money are not your family. It's business, not love. It's real life.

Another real-life money chore is paying bills. How often has your mom or dad said, "I'm the one who pays the bills around here." Wow, bill paying doesn't sound like much fun. We've seen our parents pay bills, and now Arthur pays bills of his own. But that's part of real life, too, so it's important to learn some of these things.

Money & work

Most of our money will come from the work we do each day. That means we exchange our time for money.

When you look for any job, be sure that you really want it and that you think you would be good at it. Once you are hired, be clear about what you are supposed to do. If you are working for someone, get a job description. Try to sit down before your first day of work and actually write down what is expected of you, as explained by the employer. Show him or her what you think the job is about. This helps a lot as the job goes on. It also makes you less confused and nervous about starting out. If you are offering a service or in other ways working at your own business, you should also have an understanding with your customers.

Here are some basic things to do:

$ **If you have a job now,** write down what you think is expected of you. See what your parents think of how you describe your job.

$ **Have a clear and definite deal.** Before work is started, know when and how much you will be paid.

$ **Please the boss.** Do a good job. Pay attention to the extra things the boss needs, and try to do them.

$ **Send a bill.** Here's an example:

Invoice Dated May 2, 2006
RE: Lawn mowing at
1705 Maple Road for
the week of April 25–May 2
Balance Due: $20.00
Please Pay Immediately
Late Charge 25¢ per Week

Get a raise

After you have worked for a while, it may be time to ask for a raise. Maybe you have already made a deal to get one by a certain date. But if you haven't, you'll have to ask.

Sometimes that's hard to do because you'll feel bad if the boss says no. Here are some hints to make it easier:

- **$** Don't think the boss won't like you if you ask.

- **$** Don't ask when the boss is busy.

- **$** Know how much of a raise you want.

- **$** If the boss says no, ask for a little less.

- **$** If the boss still says no, say, "Okay, we will talk about it again next month." And bring it up again.

The easiest way to get a raise is to think of some extra work to do for the boss, something you see that he, she, or the business needs. Doing something for others is the best way to get something back for yourself.

What are some things you notice that are not getting done? Are they things you can do? Can you get extra pay for doing those things?

How hard is it for you to ask for money or a raise?

Answer these questions for yourself. There are no right or wrong answers.

- **$** Do you feel awkward asking for a raise?

- **$** How much more do you want?

- **$** Is the amount based on what others earn? How did you pick the figure?

- **$** Do you feel you are doing a good job?

- **$** How will you feel if your boss says no?

$ Are you on good terms with your boss?

If you feel undeserving or ashamed to ask for money, you probably won't get paid what you are worth. Once you understand your own feelings, you can practice asking.

A word about jobs

We are both at different stages when it comes to jobs. Arthur has had a job for a few years now (since graduating college), and Rose just started working at a sandwich shop. But she's always thinking of ways to be self-employed. Most kids are self-employed because the child labor laws forbid them to be hired on a regular basis. There are many ways that we can earn money anyway. Here are a few of them:

$ Put up a lemonade stand.

$ Find ways to make money around the house or yard. For example, collect leaves and other things from your backyard, make compost, and sell it as fertilizer.

$ Buy ice at your local grocery store, crush it, and pour different types of juices on it in cups. Guess what? You've made slushies. Sell them in front of your home.

There are many ups and downs to being self-employed. Here are some of the pros: You will never have to ask your boss for a raise, because you'll be the boss. That's what self-employed means—being your own boss. And you can make your own schedule.

Now, some cons: Some self-employed people don't keep

Things to Do

Ask your mom and dad about their first jobs.

$ Was it a summer job?

$ What did they do?

$ How much were they paid?

$ What did they do with the money they earned?

$ How old were they?

Ask your grandparents the same questions. Ask other members of your family, like your older brother or sister. Ask yourself. Compare the answers and see how things might have changed over the years.

1st job • how old • paid
What did they do with the money?

Me	Grandma
Mom	Older brother
Dad	Older sister
Grandpa	Other

strict enough rules about their business. When that happens, they tend to lose money because they haven't paid attention to what keeps their business strong.

So think as carefully about self-employment as you would about any other work. You face the risk of losing the money you put into your business, but you'll also be the one who benefits most if the business does well. When you work for someone else, they take on that risk. You have to decide for yourself whether you are willing to trade risk for freedom.

What would you do if...?

How would you handle these tough on-the-job problems?

1. The man whose lawn you mow offers you $5 extra to cross a busy street and buy him groceries. It's not part of your job, and your mom doesn't want you to cross the street.

2. You work in a store at the cash register. A customer gives you too much money by mistake and starts to walk out the door.

3. Your boss tells you "times are tough" and wants you to take less money to do the same job.

4. The lemonade stand across the street charges less money than you do but doesn't use healthy stuff. They get more business.

There are lots of approaches to all these problems. Here are a few:

1. Don't go. Politely say that your mom won't like it and might make you quit. Tell him that since you enjoy mowing the lawn, you would hate to have to leave the job.

2. Call the customer back, and give him his change. Money gotten the wrong way never does you any good for long.

3. If you like your job or if other jobs are hard to find, offer to do any extra chores for the same pay. If that's not possible, offer to work for less for two weeks and then review the situation. Meanwhile, look around for other jobs.

Inside left sign:
More delicious
More nutritious
and only 5¢
more

Inside right sign:
Would you
pay 5¢ more
for a healthy
body?

4. It's time to advertise. Let everyone know they get what they pay for.

A word about allowances

You'd think that in a book about money for kids, there would be tons of stuff about allowances. Get real. A study showed that most kids get a $7 weekly allowance, and that number hasn't changed in years.

Most kids just get money in a helter-skelter way, or they nag their folks for stuff. Before you are a teenager, that's not so bad. Where do you and your family stand in the allowance picture?

$ Do you get an allowance?

$ If you do, when was the last time you got an increase?

$ Who decides whether you should get an increase now?

$ Do you keep a budget? (Show one to your parents when you ask for an increase. They'll be impressed.)

$ If you don't have a budget, do you feel you need one?

$ How do you get stuff? Do your parents buy it? Do your grandparents give you gifts?

$ Do you get enough stuff?

$ Does your brother or sister get more?

To talk to your parents about unfairness or a need you have, use what you learned earlier in this book about wishes, goals, and plans. If you have a goal, your parents may help you reach it. If you just want more stuff, they will probably say no.

Let the whole family give their views on allowances.

Daniel's allowance

Fifteen-year-old Daniel did not get an allowance, but his parents bought him everything he wanted or needed. They bought him games and food, and they also gave him money for going out with his friends.

One day during dinner, Daniel's parents asked him: "Which way would you rather do things—let us buy you all the things you need, or let us give you $25 a week as an allowance?"

Daniel wasn't sure what to choose. He thought all through dinner. At the end of dinner, he had an answer. He chose to have his parents buy him everything he needed. He decided that $25 might not cover his expenses. Daniel wasn't prepared for the goal setting and budgeting needed to manage an allowance.

Which would you have chosen, and why? What can Daniel's parents do to make him more independent and feel more capable of managing his money?

CHAPTER 19

$

Paying bills

- - - - - - - - - - - - -

Pay on time and avoid late charges.

Pablo Payment

Like most other kids, you may spend money as soon as you get it. But sometimes you may buy something that you pay for later on, usually at the end of the month. The person you pay sends a bill, like the one you may send for your work. These bills are all part of your expenses and should be in your budget.

PAYING BILLS

Most people pay all their bills at the same time every month. Some of them are tax deductible (see chapter 21), so you need to keep records. Others aren't, but you need to keep a record of payment in case someone says you did not pay. Typical bills that most grown-ups and some kids pay are

- **$** telephone bill
- **$** fuel bill
- **$** credit card bill
- **$** mortgage
- **$** electric bill, called a utility bill

The best way to keep track and to make payments is to pay by check.

You can open a checking account with your bank. Most of these accounts don't pay interest, and they are not investments. They are for convenience, record keeping, and safety in bill paying.

As proof that you have money in your checking account, the bank will give you a checkbook. Every time you write out a check, you must deduct the amount from the balance in the account. In Moneytalk, this is called *balancing the checkbook.* Grown-ups make a big deal about this. Here's why:

- **$** If the math is wrong and you write checks for more than the money in the account, the bank charges a big penalty.

- **$** If the bank makes a math mistake, it's a pain to get it corrected.

$ If you forget to write down and deduct an amount you wrote, you get **overdrawn.** The bank can also charge you a big penalty for this mistake.

So this is the simplest way we've found to balance your checkbook. Arthur learned it from his fifth-grade teacher, Ms. Delaney, at the Maplewood Middle School in Maplewood, New Jersey.

How to balance a checkbook

Balancing a checkbook is very important to good banking and to general money management. Before learning about balancing a checkbook, take a good look at a check.

Arthur Berg Bochner

④March 2, 2007   ⑦101
16-24/33467

PAY TO THE ① ShopRite Grocery Store $ ②89.93

③Eighty-Nine and 93/100 ————— DOLLARS

First City Bank
Venice Branch 063
4532 Main Street
Venice, CA 90210   ⑥ *Arthur B. Bochner*

Memo ⑤Groceries

⑈122000661⑈0526⑈063⑈723-213396

---

1. Who are you making the check out to? Write down his, her, or a company's name. If you make it out to "Cash," you are making it out to anyone who gets hold of the check.

2. The amount of the check is written in numbers. This is the amount that will be deducted from your checking account and the amount the recipient will get from a bank when it is deposited.

3. The amount of the check is written in words here.

4. The date the check is made out is written here.

5. This is the **memo,** a note to yourself and the person you write the check out to about what you are paying for. In this case, it is groceries. It could be babysitting, a different service, a product, or even a bill. In fact, if you are paying a bill, write the bill number here. You will find it on the **invoice.** See chapter 18.

6. Add your signature. The check is not good without it.

7. This is the check number. This helps you keep good records and prove you paid if someone says you didn't.

Balancing a checkbook is easy, once you get the hang of it. Let's look at an example.

Let's say you have $1,000.00 in your checking account. You go to ShopRite for groceries. The bill comes out to $89.93, so you decide to pay by check. Before you write your check, you should go to your balance sheet. First you fill in the date. Then note to whom you wrote the check; then write down the check number, located on the top right-hand side. Then you will see plus and minus signs. Circle the one that you want; in this case, it's a minus because you are giving money to the store. Then subtract your $89.93 from your $1,000.00. You get $910.07; this is your balance. Always write your checks in pen and fill out your balance sheet in pen. When you make a deposit, do the exact same thing, but circle the plus sign instead of the minus.

Checks are a great way to pay bills, but you must keep track of the account balance. If you don't, the bank will refuse to give the money to the recipient and will also charge you a fee. This is called *bouncing a check*. It will embarrass you, cost you money, and annoy the person who expects to get paid. It also will hurt your credit score and ability to borrow money in the future.

Your bank may also keep your records online for you to access. Some banks even put copies of your written checks online. Use the Internet together with the handwritten records you keep to make sure you and the bank agree on the numbers.

Date	Number	To/From	Amount/Balance
3/2/07	101	ShopRite groceries	+ $ 89.93 910.07
3/3/07	102	Toys 'R' Us Nintendo	+ $ 30.00 880.07
3/4/07	X	Boss—John Smith Paycheck	$ - 300.00 1180.07
3/5/07	103	Boys Electronics Radio	+ $ 150.00 1030.07
3/6/07	104	United Airlines Plane Tickets—LA	+ $ 139.00 891.07
3/7/07	105	Hilton Hotels Suite/room service	+ $ 120.00 771.07

Check and debit cards

In addition to your checkbook, your bank may give you a *check card* or *debit card*. These cards look just like credit cards, and they allow you to buy things (or get cash out of an automatic teller machine, or ATM) using the funds in your checking account without actually having to write a check. Every time you use the card and sign for a purchase or enter your personal access code to get cash, the money you've spent gets taken right out of your account.

These cards can be convenient, allowing you to buy things at places that don't accept checks or helping you get cash without having to go to the bank. But because they're so convenient, they can also make you more likely to spend money. They can often make it harder for you to keep track of how much you've spent, too. After all, it's easy to forget a purchase when you've only needed to sign a receipt, but it's hard to forget a purchase when you've spent time writing a check. Remember that every time you use the card, it's just like writing a check. Make sure you get a receipt every time you make a purchase, and at the end of the day, balance your checkbook the same way you would if you'd written a check. Oh, and if you get cash out of an ATM, know that you'll pay a fee for doing so if it's not a branch of your own bank.

Riddle

Q. Why is a baseball fly-out like a good check?

A. Neither of them bounces.

PART 5

$

Money matters for older kids

> Things are different for the class of 2025.

Last year, Rose (who at the time was about to turn fourteen) was allowed to attend a business camp that is part of the Foundation for Free Enterprise because our mom taught there. Most of the other kids were fifteen years old. All of them were really worried about going to college. Rose has been

You're never too young to pay taxes.

hearing about college and its cost for as long as she can remember, and Arthur is still paying off some of the loans he and our parents took out to help pay for his schooling.

For some kids, college time is right around the corner—and tuition is getting more expensive all the time. When our parents were college age, attending college cost much less than it does today. Now, most parents seem very concerned about the costs.

Chapter 20 has information on getting aid, grants, and scholarships. That's pretty important for the older kids. Age fifteen is the right time to start looking into these programs—but you should start saving *now*, no matter how old you are.

And whether you go to college or not, as long as you make any money, you'll have to pay your taxes. In fact, starting at age fourteen, kids get their own tax bracket (before that age, kids pay taxes at their parents' rate). We'll talk more about that in chapter 21. Right now, Rose's tax bracket is the same as our parents', but it won't be for long. She'll be a taxpayer before she can drive or vote!

CHAPTER 20

$

Getting to college

- - - - - - - - - - -

I'm glad my money know-how paid off.

Arnold Almost Adult

One of the biggest worries for a lot of kids is how they'll pay for attending college. It's very expensive, and tuition (the price a school charges for attending) is growing.

For example, in 2004, the average cost of a private college education was $20,045. In 2005, it was $21,235—that's a 5.9

percent increase! Public schools are much cheaper (around $5,000 a year), but their costs are rising faster than private schools' are. And these figures don't even include the costs of books, food, and living expenses. No wonder parents across the country are worried about paying for their kids' education. Four years of college can cost more than $100,000!

But there are things you and your parents can do right now to make sure you can afford whatever school you go to. *Anyone who wants to go to college can, no matter how much money he or she has.* None of us could prance into a college and pay with pocket change. Still, there are opportunities if you know how to find them. Through savings, loans, work-study programs, and smart investing, you can afford whatever colleges you get accepted to.

Don't let the numbers scare you

When our parents were our age, college was a lot cheaper. Mostly, if they got good grades, they could go. So they think that everyone must go right from high school to college and that tuition will cover most of our expenses once we get there. But this old approach may be impossible for us. When we looked at the numbers, we discovered other facts.

In a public school only half the total cost of an education goes for tuition; in a private school, 75 percent does. About 5 percent goes for books and labs. The rest goes for room and board. (*Board* means food.) So we can save some costs if we carefully choose where we'll live while in college and if we don't go overboard on a fancy lifestyle.

Under "Books and Games" you'll find books with great ideas to help you think in new ways about how to get to college.

Our top six best bets for getting to college

1. Get all the information you can by the time you are fifteen. Here's what to do: Go to your high school's guidance office, and get their material on loans, grants, scholarships, and other aid. Go to the financial aid offices at the colleges you like, and get their aid information. Look up your nearest U.S. Department of Education office in the phone book and ask for their materials. Really read this material, together with the books listed in Books and Games, to learn about every way you can get money for college. This is a full-year project at least. Start early.

2. Get a Stafford Loan. This is a government loan we can all get no matter how much money our folks have. You can get from $2,625 to $10,500 a year this way (up to a total of $46,000), depending on what year of school you need the money for and whether your parents can pay.

3. Get a Pell Grant. If your parents' income is below a certain level, you can get from $400 to $4,050 a year for college.

4. Get an associate's degree first. You can go to a two-year college, which is much less expensive, and get an associate's degree. Then you can shift into a four-year college and end up with a bachelor's degree for almost half the price of attending only the four-year college. This works because the four-year college will accept all or most of the credits you have already accumulated.

5. Join one of the armed services. You can join the armed services (such as the Army, Navy, or Air Force) and get a free college education.

6. Look for a work-study program. By participating in a work-study program you can pay your own way through college and get important job experience at the same time.

What to do with the money your parents saved for college

Some of us have money set aside for college by our parents, grandparents, or other people who care about us. A lot of Rose's friends don't know how much is saved for them. It's okay to ask about it, but don't be surprised if your folks don't want to tell you. Maybe they think that you'll want the money for something else or that you'll be disappointed if they have to use it in an emergency.

Whether they talk to you about your college savings or not, there are a few things you can help find information about that will help everyone.

$ Find out if you can prepay tuition. Some private colleges will let you prepay the tuition at any age. If you don't go, you get your money back. Since tuition is slated to increase each year, you can pay to attend school many years from now at today's cost.

$ Find out if your state has a prepayment plan. A few states will also let you prepay the public school costs. This can be a real bargain.

$ Remind your folks that 35 percent of your savings will be counted by the folks who decide if you qualify for aid, but that only 5.6 percent of their savings will be counted. Lots of folks think it's nice to put savings in an account under the kid's name, but doing this can actually hurt your chances for aid.

$ Help your parents fill out the Free Application for Federal Student Aid, or FAFSA form. You must complete this to get many types of scholarships or other aid for tuition. Complete and send it by the earliest submission date, because the sooner you send your form, the earlier you'll know how much you're getting.

$ Encourage your parents to visit a financial planner as soon as they are ready to save for your college, or to use the Web to **find what's called a 529 plan for your state.** The different 529 plans allow you to save money for college, and any growth is completely tax-free if you use the money for tuition.

$ If your parents use a credit card, see if the company has a U-Promise savings plan. If so, a small amount of what they spend using the credit card will be put into a college savings account for you.

Finally, by the time you are fifteen, work with your parents to learn all the rules that apply to college education and funding. Be flexible about your goals, and then make plans. While there's not much that younger kids can do to help out, it doesn't hurt to get good grades and to tell your parents that college is important to you.

CHAPTER 21

$

Now that you've made some money, it's time to pay your taxes

Now that you've got money, it's time to pay taxes.

Taxes are money that a government collects from its citizens to use to run the government. In the United States, we pay taxes according to how much income we make every year. April 15 is tax day. It is our responsibility to file a tax return that shows what we've earned from work and investments. We then reduce this total amount by any expenses or other money that the law lets us deduct (subtract) from our earnings. Then, we use a tax table to calculate our tax. Finally, we pay.

The U.S. Government's totally awesome tax system

O ur tax system is amazing because it is voluntary. We fill out our own forms, do our own math, and send in the money to the government's tax-collecting agency. If we want to, we can instruct our employers to send some of our money to the tax collector as we get paid during the year. This is called *tax withholding,* and it makes it easier to pay up when the time comes. Depending on how many dependents (people who you support) you tell the employer you have, he or she will withhold more or less from your paychecks. Having more dependents results in less money being withheld.

Some people don't pay, don't fill out the form correctly, or don't pay the right amount in taxes. When this happens, the tax collector has the right to review the taxpayer's papers. This review is called an *audit.* If the tax collector thinks the taxpayer is wrong, the taxpayer may have to pay a fine or a penalty in addition to the rest of their taxes. Still, there is a Taxpayer's Bill of Rights that allows a taxpayer to take the case to a court and to have the audit in a convenient place. The Taxpayer's Bill of Rights also gives other kinds of protection from abuse.

By the way, the U.S. government's tax collector is called the *Internal Revenue Service (IRS),* and the tax law is called the *Internal Revenue Code.*

How much tax will you pay?

The amount of taxes you pay is based on two things: (1) the amount of money you made during the year and (2) the money you can deduct from that total before you must figure out your final tax. Most people pay local, state, and federal taxes. Federal taxes, the biggest of them all, change often. We now have five graduated rates, ranging from 15.0 percent to 39.6 percent. The more money you make, the more taxes you are responsible for. Married couples pay a little differently. And new tax laws may change all these percentages soon.

As for the things you can deduct, there are so many it's hard to make a list. Here are some important ones:

- **$** **Expenses related to making money,** such as travel, stationery, and secretarial pay

- **$** **The cost of doctors** and medicine if you are sick

- **$** **Other taxes** (except sales taxes) you paid to the state in which you live or for the land taxes on your house

- **$** **Interest that you paid to the bank** if you have a mortgage

How can you tell whether you're paying the right amount of tax?

Under the Taxpayer's Bill of Rights, every citizen is allowed to pay as little tax as is legitimately possible. That's why the most important thing you should do to save on taxes is keep good records. After all, it's not possible to take all the deductions if you can't remember what you spent. Every time you forget to take a deduction or you can't prove it to the IRS, you lose money.

Investing to save taxes

Choosing tax-safe investments can help you pay less taxes. Let's look at two possibilities. With the first one, you'll never be taxed; with the second, you'll pay taxes on a delayed schedule.

One way to save taxes is to invest in *municipal bonds*. These are loans you make to a city or state in return for interest payments (see chapter 8). Because of the U.S. Constitution, the federal government can't tax you on money you have earned from lending to state or city governments. The signers of the Constitution wanted to prevent the government from taxing loans that the citizens make to it, because they thought such taxes would be a way for the federal government to keep the states poor and take over their power.

A different kind of tax-wise investment is called *tax deferral,* in Moneytalk. The word *deferred* is really just a fancy way of saying *delayed* or *later.* With tax-deferred accounts, you don't get taxed on the money they earn. Meanwhile, the earnings and profits keep getting reinvested without any taxes being taken out.

Having this kind of account makes a big difference in how much you end up with. For example, if you invested $2,000 every year, earning 9 percent interest in the 31 percent tax bracket, at the end of twenty-five years you would have $184,648 if the investment was tax deferred, instead of $120,049 if it was not deferred.

The cool thing is that even kids can use these special tax-deferred accounts. Many people don't know that. If you earn money, you can put up to $4,000 a year in an account called an *individual retirement account,* or *IRA* (that limit will go up soon). That's what Arthur did with the money he made from the first edition of this book.

The kiddie tax: No kidding

Don't think that you don't have to pay taxes just because you are a kid. You do. There is a *kiddie tax* (we hate that phrase). And it doesn't matter how young you are, as long as you earn money from work or make money from investing. You've probably seen those babies in the tire commercials on TV. They get paid for jumping around in diapers, and they have to pay taxes on the money they make. Their parents or a guardian must file a tax return for them.

But if a kid has money from profits or interest, not from working, there is a different rule that involves the kiddie tax. For money you earn by investing (not from work), up to the time you are fourteen—starting in 2010, up to age eighteen (we told you earlier that tax laws change)—you pay the same percentage of your income as your parents pay of theirs. The percentage of your income that you must pay in taxes is called your *tax bracket,* in Moneytalk. So if your parents pay 15 percent, so do you.

Once you reach age fourteen (eighteen in 2010), you get your own tax bracket. You probably don't make much, so you'll be in the 15 percent bracket. But relax a little. The first

$850 you earn each year is tax free, the next $850 is taxed at your own bracket, and after that you are taxed like Mom and Dad until you reach fourteen (eighteen in 2010).

Since you will start to invest after reading this book, don't forget to tell your parents about the kiddie tax. They must fill out kiddie tax forms for you. They sign them as your guardian. Gee, we're old enough to pay taxes but not old enough to sign our own forms. Bummer.

Filing your taxes online

If you are comfortable using the Internet, you can file your taxes using one of the many companies that offer tax preparation services online. Of course, their help costs money. However, filing online has benefits. Filing online can simplify your tax returns because the computer programs make everything easy. You just answer questions and fill in amounts when the computer asks. And, as a bonus, you generally get your refund check from the government (if you've overpaid your taxes) quicker than if you filed by mail. Another great benefit is that you automatically get a receipt that is saved online. Just don't forget your username and password!

Some good online filing sites include Turbotax (www.Turbotax.com) and H&R Block (www.HRBlock.com).

Final note: How you feel about money says a lot about you

As we wrote this book, our mom kept saying, "Money is a neutral thing. It's not good or bad. It's all according to how you feel and think about it." As with many things, not everyone agrees about money matters. Maybe your folks fight about money with each other, with your brother or sister, or with you. Maybe your friends have different ideas. That's no surprise. Money is a big topic, and people feel differently about it.

What we learned about money in writing this book is that developing a money style and handling money are part of growing up. Dealing with feelings about money is also part of growing up. How you work things out says a lot about your future career, life choices, and even happiness.

When Keith, our editor, asked us to write a final chapter for the book, we looked through it to pick out the things we wanted to think more about.

Goals: What are yours?

People have different goals. Some are short term; others are long term. One may be to go to college; another may be to become a senator or a lawyer. Rose's goal in life is to be a teacher. That's a long-term goal. But she also has the short-term goal of going to the best college for aspiring teachers. By now, *you* have had time to think about *your* goals.

$ Do you have a plan to reach your goals?

To achieve a goal, you must have a plan, as we discussed in chapter 2. A plan is something that will get you somewhere or get you something. Here is an example of a goal: I want to go to college, and I need to save money to do it. Here is my plan: I will do more odd jobs around the house, and I will mow more front lawns every week. When I get the extra money, I will put it in the bank. Before long, I'm on my way.

$ Budgets: A look at Thomas

Many people have a budget, but others don't like having one. As described in chapter 3, a budget will help you organize and make a plan. Remember Thomas? He used a budget to help him get some things he wanted. What do you want your budget to do for you?

$ Money in your future

How important do you think money will be to you? Knowing about money and how to invest it doesn't mean that it has to rule our lives. Will money be prominent in your life? What kind of grown-up do you think you will be as far as money is concerned?

$ What do you consider financial success?

When will you be happy with how much money you have? That's one of the biggest questions that grown-ups have to answer. In one study our mother read about, all the adults wanted double the money they had or double the money they earned. When Rose heard this, she was very surprised. She always thought that adults were content with what they had. Obviously not. How much money do you think you will need to earn each year to be content?

$ Collector, trader, or buyer: Which are you?

As you read in chapter 12, a collector is a person who accumulates things like baseball cards, comic books, coins, or anything that will be worth something later. Then he or she sells part of the collection once in a while to get better stuff. A trader is a person who's just like a collector; but instead of buying things to trade up, he or she buys to make money. A buyer is a person who will buy the things, just as the trader or collector would, but will not sell them. He or she is a keeper. What are you—a buyer, a trader, or a collector?

$ Socially responsible investing: What do you believe in?

Socially responsible investing means that you invest in a company you believe does things the right way. In chapter 13 we talked about ways you can invest to help save the planet. As another example, you might think that testing products on animals is not right, so you wouldn't invest in companies that test on animals. What are some socially responsible things that are important to you?

$ Taxes: Do you think they are fair?

Taxes are something that everybody has to pay. You pay them to the federal and state governments every year on April 15 if you make money from working or investments. Taxes are very high. As much as 44 percent of every dollar you earn may go to taxes, depending on the tax rate of the state where you live. You keep the rest. They say that the average person works from January to May just to pay taxes. You pay taxes on many other things, like the property and the house that you own and the things that you buy. Taxes are collected so the government can spend money on things that are good for everyone. What are some of the things you think the government should spend your tax money on? When you are old enough to vote, elect people who agree with you about this.

Hey, kids, this part is just between you and me (Rose)

This is the second time I've written to you personally about this book. This time, it's about how much you have learned by reading the book. I hope you have learned many things that will help you in your life. But there is only one way to find out: *Take a test.*

I had to fight with Keith, my editor, and Arthur to keep this test in the book. They think that tests are boring and that mine will scare you away. They forget that in school we get tests with breakfast, lunch, and dinner. Bored is our middle name. So what could one more little test hurt, to see how much you know about money? At least there is no teacher grading you on it.

████ ███ ███ ███ ███ ████

1. When you look for a loan, are high interest rates good for you?

2. If you wanted to buy a stock, why would you want to know its P/E ratio?

3. If you wanted to buy a $150,000 house but you had only $60,000, what could you do?

4. What does DRIP stand for?

5. What happens to the prices of things when the government puts a tax on them? Name things that you buy that have a tax on them.

6. What is dollar cost averaging?

7. Is a mutual fund a group of stocks or a stock?

8. How does the government tax children's income? earnings from investments? Does it make a difference how old you are?

9. What does a broker do?

10. How is it possible to invest your money in a foreign country?

You probably don't know the answers to all these questions. But if you got any right, that's great. All the answers are in this book, and as you read and learn more about money, what you need to know will come easily.

Well, enjoy your financial life—and most of all, have fun!

Mom gets the last word

by Adriane G. Berg

Dear Parents,

Financial success need not mean great wealth or riches. Most of us are happiest with lifelong feelings of security and prosperity. But sometimes, as adults, it seems these feelings have eluded us. How we face our money challenges and opportunities often has more to do with our childhood experiences than our adult circumstances.

Why do some people bounce back from financial adversity to become even stronger? Why do others continually fail to make ends meet? Inner resources, coping skills, and attitudes toward money are all learned. There is nothing genetic about money except the accident of inheritance.

Whether we parents realize it, we are continually teaching our children about money. We do this through example, through our casual conversations, and through our inevitable money fights. Every time we choose a gift, give a party, or go to the movies, we have a spending event that reveals a little of our "money self" to our kids.

What our children absorb is the family money culture that forms the basis of their reaction system. You won't be surprised to learn that what you do and say has more influence on your children's response to earning, saving, investing, and thinking about money than anything else.

For instance, it can be very telling to ask your child which family he or she knows is the happiest. Find a point of reference familiar to your child. Rose watches television a great deal (tsk-tsk), so she knows all the TV families. Maybe you would prefer to use references from books or ones from real life. In any case, pick a few examples, making sure to include some that are obviously rich and poor.

Next, ask your child to associate some of these attributes with each: organized, friendly, safe, happy, loving, neat, jolly, cross, loud, sweet. You'd be surprised how often the blue-collar family in *The King of Queens* wins over more affluent families and how often the impoverished children in *Little Women* do better than the wealthy kids in *The Secret Garden*.

Unlike other topics, even sex and drugs, we rarely talk to our kids about money directly. Mostly, they learn by example and innuendo. "What kind of money baby were you?" is a question I often ask in the books I write for adults. How are your kids interpreting what they hear about work, money, and investing in the home?

How to discuss family money culture

I have ended this book with two exercises that you can do with your children informally to help you find out how they are interpreting your family's money-related talk. The first is a list of money sayings that your children hear in the home, mostly from you. You can add to the list. Then you can talk to them about what they think the sayings mean.

My purpose is to give you a method of learning, without

asking directly, how your children are developing with regard to their money personalities. No child can tell you if he or she is a saver or spender. But your children can tell you that Grandma keeps saying, "We never were allowed to have that when we were your age," and they can tell you how that makes them feel.

You can ask kids how they feel about things they hear about money and our economy in the news, in school, on TV, and in the home. Anytime we get a better understanding of how our actions and the actions of others affect our kids, we can better direct them.

The second exercise is your financial family tree. Arthur and Rose know who their ancestors were, when they immigrated to the United States, how political oppression in Europe forced them to relinquish their assets, and how each generation rebuilt.

This understanding makes them proud, even though they are not the richest people in town. Kids don't think too much about money and status until the world forces them to do so. I believe that family pride will help them see through false values better than any direct teaching from us.

Money sayings

Do you hear any of these money phrases at home? If so, who in your family says them? What do you think they mean? How do they make you feel?

- **$** "He's money mad."
- **$** "He's only out for money."

$ "Money isn't everything."

$ "She's lucky; she doesn't have to work."

$ "Money doesn't grow on trees."

$ "Money makes money."

$ "I can never understand anything about money."

$ "I've been rich, and I've been poor. Rich is better."

Family financial tree

Here is a good discussion for children to have with their parents and, even better, their grandparents.

Have your child find out if your family or any of your ancestors were rich, poor, landowners, or even royalty. Here are questions he or she might want to ask:

$ Where did my great-grandparents come from? my grandparents?

$ What kind of house did they live in?

$ Did the family's fortune ever change because of wars, bad business, or other troubles?

$ What did my great-grandparents and grandparents do for a living?

$ Are there any good stories about how a family member made lots of money?

Oh yes—even if the kids know about money, they won't confuse rich with happy. Only grown-ups do that. Just ask them.

Words that are good to know

Accountant: A professional who helps you handle your tax return and other tax-related tasks.

Banker: A bank employee who lends money and invests your deposits, securities (stocks), or bonds.

Borrowing: Using someone else's money with their permission in return for giving it back to them, sometimes with extra money for letting you use theirs.

Broker: Someone licensed to buy and sell stocks for you.

Budget: A way of keeping track of money you get and spend.

Call: The money you lent is paid back early. This can happen with a bond.

Capital: The amount of money you invest.

Certified financial planner: A professional who helps you plan and reach your financial goals.

Collateral: Stuff you will have to forfeit to someone who lends you money if you can't pay him or her back.

WORDS THAT ARE GOOD TO KNOW

Collectibles: Items you buy, such as baseball cards or artwork, with the idea of selling them someday for more than you paid.

Commission: A percentage of the cost of an investment you made that you pay to a broker for buying the investment for you. To buy some investments, you need a special license, so you can't buy them yourself.

Commodities: Anything that is traded, like agricultural products, gold, or oil, in the belief that it will be worth more later and can be sold to make money.

There are three major differences between collectibles and commodities: (1) You usually like what you collect; commodities are not important to you except to make money. (2) You usually take what you collect home; a broker just keeps a record of the commodities you buy. (3) You own collectibles for a long time; it can take some time to find a buyer. Commodities are bought and sold fast; there is always a quick market for selling through a broker.

Company: A business.

Credit: The ability to borrow money.

Debt: The obligation to pay back borrowed money.

Defaulting: Not paying back the money you borrowed.

Deposit: Money you put into an account.

Discount broker: Someone who charges lower commissions or charges you on the basis of the number of shares you buy, not their price.

WORDS THAT ARE GOOD TO KNOW

Diversification: Investing in many different things to reduce your overall risk of loss.

Dollar cost averaging: Regularly investing the same amount of money in a stock so you'll do better than if you'd invested a lot at once.

DRIP (dividend reinvestment plan): A plan that allows you to automatically buy more shares of stock with profits.

Emerging growth countries: Countries that are just beginning to have economies you can invest in.

Expenses: Your cost of living.

FDIC (Federal Deposit Insurance Corporation): A U.S. government agency set up in 1933 to pay back money you put in a bank if the bank defaults.

Global fund: A mutual fund that invests in companies in many foreign countries and in the United States.

Global investing: Investing outside of the United States.

Goal: Something you want to achieve for yourself or someone you love.

Growth: When something you buy can be sold for a higher price.

Income: Money that comes to you from anyone in any way.

Insurance agent: Someone licensed to help you buy insurance.

WORDS THAT ARE GOOD TO KNOW

Interest: Money that you are paid for lending your money to others or that you pay to others when you borrow money.

International fund: A mutual fund that invests in companies in foreign countries.

Investing: (1) Using your money to buy something that will make more money for you when you sell it or (2) lending your money to others to get interest.

IRA (individual retirement account): A retirement account where you can put in up to $4,000 per year and accumulate growth or interest on a tax-deferred basis.

Kiddie tax: A tax on the earnings from children's investments or earnings. Kids pay at their parents' rate until age eighteen, when they get their own tax bracket.

Lawyer: Someone licensed to practice law. In money matters, a lawyer often helps with tax problems.

Lend: Let others borrow your money.

Long-term goal: Something you want to achieve in the future.

Markup: The difference between what a bond costs a broker and what it is sold to you for.

Maturity date: The date when a loan must be paid back with interest.

Mutual fund: A fund that owns lots of securities and pools the money of investors to buy them. It is operated by an investment company.

Plan: A strategy to achieve a goal.

Prospectus: A disclosure document containing details about the mutual fund that issues it.

Real estate: Property such as a house or a store.

Real estate broker or agent: Someone licensed to buy and sell real estate for you.

Securities: Stocks or bonds.

Shares of stock: Units of ownership in a company.

Short-term goal: Something you want to achieve quickly.

Socially responsible investing: Investing in companies that have the values you think are good.

Stockholders' meeting: A meeting between the people who own a particular stock and the company executives, usually to vote on matters of management. The meeting takes place once a year.

Tax: Money you pay to the national, state, or city government every year on your earnings.

Tax deferred: Earnings that don't get taxed until the year in which you use the money.

Tax exempt: Earnings that never get taxed.

Tax free: Also earnings that never get taxed.

Unit: A share in a mutual fund.

Books & games

Books for kids

Alexander, Sue. *Finding Your First Job.* New York: Dutton, 1980.

Berg, Adriane G. *Your Kids, Your Money.* Englewood Cliffs, N.J.: Prentice-Hall, 1985.

Drew, Bonny. *Fast Cash for Kids.* Franklin Lakes, N.J.: Career Press, 1991.

Godfrey, Joline. *Raising Financially Fit Kids.* Berkeley, Calif.: Ten Speed Press, 2003.

Godfrey, Neale S. *Money Doesn't Grow on Trees: A Parent's Guide to Raising Financially Responsible Children.* New York: Fireside, 2006.

Harmon, Hollis Page. *Money Sense for Kids.* 2nd ed. Hauppauge, N.Y.: Barron's Educational Series, 2005.

Henry, Joanne Landers. *Bernard Baruch.* Indianapolis: Bobbs-Merrill, 1991.

Karlitz, Gail. *Growing Money: A Complete Investing Guide for Kids*. New York: Price Stern Sloan, 2001.

Mayr, Diane. *The Everything Kids' Money Book: From Saving to Spending to Investing—Learn All About Money!* Cincinnati: Adams Media Corporation, 2002.

McCurrach, David. *Allowance Magic: Turn Your Kids into Money Wizards*. Kids' Money Press, 2003.

Pearl, Jayne A. *Kids and Money: Giving Them the Savvy to Succeed Financially*. New York: Bloomberg Press, 1999.

Smith, Pat, and Lynn Roney. *Wow the Dow! The Complete Guide to Teaching Your Kids How to Invest in the Stock Market*. New York: Fireside, 2000.

United States Coin Collector's Check List. Racine, Wis.: Western Publishing Company, 1988.

Weinstein, Grace W. *Children and Money*. New York: New American Library, 1985.

Games

Bank Account Game. Creative Teaching Associates.

Big Deal Money Game. Creative Teaching Associates.

Decisions: A Stock Market Money Management Game. Creative Teaching Associates.

Games

Discount: A Consumer Math Game. Creative Teaching Associates.

Easy Money. Milton Bradley (Winning Moves).

Educational Insights Hot Dots Money Flash Cards.

I'm the Boss. Face 2 Face Games (Schmidt Spiele).

Sale—A Consumer Math Game. Creative Teaching Associates.

And the granddaddy of them all: Monopoly. Parker Brothers.

College books

Blum, Laurie. *Free Money for College.* New York: Facts on File, 1999.

Cassidy, Daniel J., and Michael J. Alves. *The Scholarship Book.* 12th ed. Englewood Cliffs, N.J.: Prentice-Hall, 2006.

McCee, Cynthia Ruiz, and Phillip C. McCee Jr. *Cash for College.* New York: Hearst Books, 1999.

Index

INDEX

INDEX

INDEX

INDEX

About the Authors

Arthur Bochner wrote *The Totally Awesome Money Book for Kids* with his mother when he was eleven years old and *The Totally Awesome Business Book for Kids* when he was thirteen. Now twenty-four, he's a political speechwriter in Washington, D.C.

Rose Bochner, Arthur's fifteen-year-old sister, was nominated for the Distinguished Students Award at her New Jersey middle school. She's a rock climber and plans to teach.

Adriane G. Berg is a renowned speaker, attorney, and leader in the field of finance and aging. She is the author of a dozen books on personal finance—the wife of Stuart (Spendthrift) Bochner and the mother of Arthur and Rose.

MORE NEWMARKET PRESS BOOKS FOR YOUNG READERS

TOTALLY AWESOME BOOKS BY ARTHUR BOCHNER AND ROSE BOCHNER

The New Totally Awesome Money Book for Kids
Named by the *American Library Association* as a "Best Book of the Year," this popular guide for 8- to 14-year-olds includes quizzes, games, forms, charts, stories, and drawings on the basics of saving, investing, borrowing, working, and taxes.
192 pages. Drawings. Glossary. Index. 5 $\frac{3}{16}$" x 8". 978-1-55704-738-0. $9.95. Paperback.

The New Totally Business Business Book for Kids
This fun, fact-filled guide for 8- to 14-year-olds includes quizzes, games, cartoons, and all the information a young person needs to know about starting up a business.
192 pages. Drawings. Glossary. Index. 5 $\frac{3}{16}$" x 8". 978-1-55704-757-1. $9.95. Paperback.

THE JUNIOR SU DOKU SERIES
Created especially for kids ages 8 and up, each edition boasts over 110 puzzles that involve numbers, words, and shapes, ranging from easy 4 x 4 grids to the more challenging 6 x 6 and classic 9 x 9 puzzles.

Junior Su Doku
112 pages. 122 puzzles. 5 $\frac{3}{16}$" x 8 $\frac{1}{4}$". 978-1-55704-706-9. $4.95. Paperback.

Junior Su Doku Valentine's Day
With Valentine's Day–themed words and shapes!
128 pages. 136 puzzles. 5 $\frac{3}{16}$" x 8 $\frac{1}{4}$". 978-1-55704-713-7. $4.95. Paperback.

Junior Su Doku Easter
With Easter-themed words and shapes!
128 pages. 136 puzzles. 5 $\frac{3}{16}$" x 8 $\frac{1}{4}$". 978-1-55704-715-1. $4.95. Paperback.

Junior Su Doku Halloween
With Halloween–themed words and shapes!
128 pages. 130 puzzles. 5 $\frac{3}{16}$" x 8 $\frac{1}{4}$". 978-1-55704-730-4. $4.95. Paperback.

Junior Su Doku Christmas
With Christmas–themed words and shapes!
128 pages. 111 puzzles. 5 $\frac{3}{16}$" x 8 $\frac{1}{4}$". 978-1-55704-707-6. $4.95. Paperback.

Kidoku
The ultimate puzzle book for kids, featuring five different kinds of puzzles and logic games including Su Doku.
224 pages. 204 puzzles. 5 $\frac{3}{16}$" x 8 $\frac{1}{4}$". 978-1-55704-720-5. $6.95. Paperback.

FICTION FOR YOUNG READERS

Akeelah and the Bee
A Novel by James W. Ellison
Based on the screenplay by Doug Atchison
An inspirational drama about Akeelah Anderson, a precocious 11-year-old girl from South Los Angeles with a gift for words.
192 pages. 5 ¼" x 8". 978-1-55704-729-8. $6.95. Paperback.

Finding Forrester
A Novel by James W. Ellison
Based on the screenplay by Mike Rich
The inspiring story of the unlikely friendship between a famous, reclusive novelist and an amazingly gifted teen who secretly yearns to be a writer.
192 pages. 5 ¼" x 8". 978-1-55704-479-2. $9.95. Paperback.

Fly Away Home
A Novel by Patricia Hermes
Based on the Screenplay Written by Robert Rodat and Vince McKewin
Adapted from the film by the award-winning author of *Kevin Corbett Eats Flies* and *My Girl*, this inspirational family adventure follows 14-year-old Amy and her inventor father as they attempt to teach geese how to fly.
160 pages. 5 ³⁄₁₆" x 7 ⅝". 978-1-55704-489-1. $7.95. Paperback.

Two Brothers: The Tales of Kumal and Sangha
A Novel by James W. Ellison
Based on the Screenplay by Alain Godard & Jean-Jacques Annaud
Inspired by the acclaimed family film from the maker of *The Bear*, a heartwarming nature tale about two tiger cubs born in the Southeast Asian jungle.
192 pages. 5 ³⁄₁₆" x 7 ⅝". 978-1-55704-489-1. $7.95. Paperback.

THREE CLASSIC WILDERNESS TALES BY JAMES OLIVER CURWOOD

The Bear
Thor, a mighty grizzly, and Muskwa, a motherless bear cub, become companions in the Canadian wilderness in this exciting story that inspired the film *The Bear.*
208 pages. 5 ³⁄₁₆" x 7 ⅝". 978-1-55704-131-9. $5.95. Paperback.

Baree, The Story of a Wolf-Dog
The thrilling "timeless tale" (*ALA Booklist*) of a half-tame, half-wild wolf pup who must survive alone in the Canadian wilderness.
256 pages. 5 ³⁄₁₆" x 7 ⅝". 978-1-55704-132-6. $5.95. Paperback.

Kazan, Father of Baree
The truly unforgettable story of Kazan, the mightiest canine of the Canadian wilderness.
240 pages. 5 ³⁄₁₆" x 7 ⅝". 978-1-55704-225-5. $5.95. Paperback.

THE "WHAT'S HAPPENING TO MY BODY?" SERIES
THE BESTSELLING GUIDES FOR PRETEENS AND TEENS
BY LYNDA MADARAS AND AREA MADARAS

The "What's Happening to My Body?" Book for Girls

This classic book covers the body's changing size and shape, breasts, the reproductive organs, the menstrual cycle, pubic hair, puberty in boys, diet, exercise, health, and much more.

304 pages. Drawings. Index. 6 $\frac{1}{8}$" x 9 $\frac{1}{8}$".

978-1-55704-764-9. $12.95. Paperback • 978-1-55704-768-7. $24.95. Hardcover.

The "What's Happening to My Body?" Book for Boys

The classic puberty education book for boys covers the body's changing size and shape, hair, voice changes, perspiration, pimples, the reproductive organs, sexuality, puberty in girls, and much more.

272 pages. Drawings. Index. 6 $\frac{1}{8}$" x 9 $\frac{1}{8}$".

978-1-55704-765-6. $12.95. Paperback • 978-1-55704-769-4. $24.95. Hardcover.

My Body, My Self for Girls

Fun and fact-filled—over 100 quizzes, checklists, games, and journal pages about your changing body.

128 pages. Illustrations. Index. 6 $\frac{1}{8}$" x 9 $\frac{1}{8}$". 978-1-55704-766-3. $12.95. Paperback.

My Body, My Self for Boys

Fun and fact-filled—over 100 quizzes, checklists, games, and journal pages about your changing body.

112 pages. Illustrations. Index. 6 $\frac{1}{8}$" x 9 $\frac{1}{8}$". 978-1-55704-767-0. $12.95. Paperback.

Ready, Set, Grow!
A "What's Happening to My Body?" Book for Younger Girls

Written especially for 8–11-year-old girls and playfully illustrated with lively cartoon drawings, *Ready, Set, Grow!* covers all the new and exciting changes girls can expect.

128 pages. Illustrations. Index. 7" x 7".

978-1-55704-565-2. $12.00. Paperback • 978-1-55704-587-4. $22.00. Hardcover.

For postage and handling, please add $5.00 for the first book, plus $1.50 for each additional book. Prices and availability are subject to change. Please call 800-669-3903 to place a credit card order.

I enclose a check or money order payable to **Newmarket Press** in the amount of $ _____

Name _____

Address _____

City/State/Zip _____

E-mail Address _____

For discounts on orders of five or more copies or to get a catalog, contact Newmarket Press, Special Sales Department, 18 East 48th Street, New York, NY 10017; phone 212-832-3575 or 800-669-3903; fax 212-832-3629; or e-mail sales@newmarketpress.com

www.newmarketpress.com   NewTotallyAwesomeMoney07.qxp